T0129368

Also by John Sager

Nonfiction

A Tiffany Monday—An Unusual Love Story, WestBow Press, 2012

Joan's Gallery, 50 Years of Artistry by Joan Kohl Johnson Sager, Blurb, Inc., 2013

Uncovered—My Half-Century with the CIA, WestBow Press, 2013

Sasha, from Stalin to Obama (biography), Create Space, 2016

The Conservator (biography), Create Space, 2017

Fiction

Night Flight, Create Space, 2013

Operation Night Hawk, Create Space, 2014

Moscow at Midnight, Create Space, 2014

The Jihadists' Revenge, Create Space, 2014

Mole, 2015

Capital Crises, Create Space, 2015

God's Listeners (anthology), Create Space, 2015

Crescent Blood, Create Space, 2016

Shahnoza—Super Spy, Create Space, 2016

Target: Oahu, Create Space, 2017

Aerosol, Create Space, 2017

The Health Center, Create Space, 2017

The Evil Alliance, Create Space, 2018

Tehran
Revisited
A Novel

John Sager

ARCHWAY
PUBLISHING

Copyright © 2019 John Sager.

All rights reserved. No part of this book may be used or reproduced by any means, graphic, electronic, or mechanical, including photocopying, recording, taping or by any information storage retrieval system without the written permission of the author except in the case of brief quotations embodied in critical articles and reviews.

This is a work of fiction. All of the characters, names, incidents, organizations, and dialogue in this novel are either the products of the author's imagination or are used fictitiously.

Archway Publishing books may be ordered through booksellers or by contacting:

Archway Publishing
1663 Liberty Drive
Bloomington, IN 47403
www.archwaypublishing.com
1 (888) 242-5904

Because of the dynamic nature of the Internet, any web addresses or links contained in this book may have changed since publication and may no longer be valid. The views expressed in this work are solely those of the author and do not necessarily reflect the views of the publisher, and the publisher hereby disclaims any responsibility for them.

Any people depicted in stock imagery provided by Getty Images are models, and such images are being used for illustrative purposes only. Certain stock imagery © Getty Images.

ISBN: 978-1-4808-7369-8 (sc)
ISBN: 978-1-4808-7370-4 (e)

Library of Congress Control Number: 2019930173

Print information available on the last page.

Archway Publishing rev. date: 1/11/2019

Cast of Characters

(In alphabetical order)

Adam Cartwright, Deputy Director for Operations, Central Intelligence Agency

David Franklin, Director, Central Intelligence Agency

Nicholas Jackson, DCOS Ashkhabad station

Ali Khamenei, Supreme Leader, Islamic Republic if Iran

Habib Khamenei, Ali Khamenei's son

Hussein Khamenei, Ali Khamenei's grandson

Roya Khamenei, Ali Khamenei's granddaughter

Jeff Khavari, CIA case officer assigned to Headquarters

Anthony (Tony) Matthews, CIA Chief of Station, Beirut

Abdul Nazari, American national, CIA deep cover asset

Suzanne Nazari, Abdul's wife

Owen Oglethorpe, president of the United States

Farhad Rafati, Iranian counselor/psychologist, CIA deep cover asset

Thomas Russell, Chief of Station, Ashkhabad, Turkmenistan

Abdullah Safavi, Iranian national, CIA deep cover asset

Sanaz Safavi, Abdulla's grandmother

Mustafa Shadid, Lebanese national, Beirut station asset

Hadar Sohrab, Deputy Director, VAJA

Esfir Sohrab, Hadar's daughter

Sam Wolters, Chief, Near East Division, CIA Headquarters

Ali Younesi, Director, VAJA

Thomas Zimmerman, Wolters's deputy

Glossary

(in alphabetical order)

Bigot List: In intelligence service parlance, a list of names of persons who are aware of a particular operation. Such lists are called for when the operation is of high value or high sensitivity, or both.

DDO: The Deputy Director for Operations. The directorate is also known as the Clandestine Service. The DDO is the third-highest ranking officer in the CIA, and his appointment requires White House approval.

EEIs: Essential Elements of Information. In intelligence service parlance, those bits of intelligence (information) that are important to an agent's service. What are the specific things he should look for? Some are more important than others, and the agent may have to make decisions that are critical to the success of the mission.

NSA: The National Security Agency. Headquartered at Fort Meade, Maryland, the NSA is responsible for the collection and analysis of all sigint (signals intelligence) data, primarily from earth satellites. Cybersecurity is another NSA responsibility, one only recently levied by the U.S. Congress.

Rial (ree-AL): The Iranian currency. When I served in Iran in the 1950s, one US dollar bought 76 rials. Today, one US dollar buys 128,000 rials, making it virtually without value.

RID: Records Integration Division. Ever since 1948, one year after the establishment of the CIA, its Records Integration Division has been the primary "intelligence library" for the Agency. Every report, no matter the source, goes to RID for cataloguing and indexing. It is primarily used as a source of information on individual persons: name, gender, date and place of birth, and whatever other biographical information is useful. Over its many years, RID's database approaches that of the Library of Congress, some 500 terabytes of information.

SRAC: Sort Range Agent Communicator. A device which broadcasts an encoded voice message with such speed as to make it undetectable by a hostile intelligence service. The person receiving the message uses a decoding device that converts the message to audible speech.

VAJA. The Iranian intelligence service. Responsible for internal security and overseas espionage. Established in 1984, the organization has coequal status among Iran's other ministries and is known to have been responsible, in its early stages, for the assassinations of dissidents.

Walk-in. A person who voluntarily agrees to cooperate with, or work for, an intelligence agency.

Acknowledgment

As with many of my previous writings I am once again indebted to my longtime fly fishing friend, Stanford Young. Stan has perused the entire manuscript, and any glitches, typos, and other flubs are my errors, not his. Thanks again, Stan!

Prologue

The Oval Office, Monday, 1100 hours, June 18, 2018

President Oglethorpe has excused CIA Director David Franklin after giving him a most unusual assignment: bring about regime change in Iran, and do it so that it appears to be an internal coup d'état, i.e., no American fingerprints. And do it before Khamenei dies. He is seventy-nine years old, so the available window may be no more than a year.

Oglethorpe recently has returned from his summit meeting in Singapore with North Korea's leader, Kim Jong-un, and his at-home political fortunes have never looked brighter. He reasons, with some justification, that even if his operation in Tehran should fail, his Republican base will understand and forgive. Therefore, bringing about regime change in Iran is well worth the risk. He expects the CIA to succeed within the year.

This is the story of how that operation unfolded, as much as can now be told.

One

The travel office had told Jeff Khavari he could save the Agency a few dollars by staying at the Bellevue Holiday Inn, and that's how his travel orders were written, even though it meant taking the red-eye from Dulles International to SeaTac. Word had come from the White House a week before that every executive agency in Oglethorpe's orbit should reduce its spending by no less than 10 percent. "Draining the swamp" meant, among other things, spending less on travel and the perks that went with it.

As soon as he walked out of baggage claim, Jeff retrieved his iPhone and tapped the Uber icon; the car arrived five minutes later.

* * *

Jeff had never visited the Pacific Northwest. This would be a new experience. He had compiled a list of names, names extracted from the Agency's two billion gigabyte database. Each of them appeared in typewritten Farsi, and that helped because the Agency was short on help and employed only a few native Farsi speakers who could read and write the language. Beside each name was an address, a phone number, the age of the target, and as much as was known of the target's employment history. One name in particular intrigued him. He decided to begin there.

Before leaving headquarters, Jeff had done the research. Who were the leaders of the Bellevue area Iranian expatriate community? How old was each of them, and how often did they meet? He knew that the group thought of themselves as "royalists," hoping that someday their hero could return to Tehran and resume his rightful place on the Peacock Throne. But it was not to be. Reza Pahlavi, the Shah's only surviving son, was living in Bethesda, Maryland, and he no longer had the ear of nearby members of Congress or the local media reps. Jeff had considered calling the man, perhaps to ask for an endorsement, but he thought better of it. According to Reza Pahlavi's 201 file, it had been five years since anyone from the Agency had spoken to him.

He checked into his room, took the escalator to the ground floor, and walked into a coffee shop that advertised In and Out in Ten Minutes. The menu told him what he was looking for: black coffee, two soft-boiled eggs on wheat toast with butter and orange marmalade, and a side of Virginia ham. Next step: the phone call.

Two

His name was Abdul Nazari, age thirty, divorced, no kids, a former Bellevue High basketball star, fluent in Farsi, Arabic, and his birth tongue—American English—and head of his section at Microsoft's Bellevue office. Jeff had learned this and running a routine name trace on his target before leaving headquarters. He found Nazari's number in his iPhone's contacts list, tapped the icon, and waited. Three rings later:

"Hi, this is Abdul. I'm away from my phone right now, but if you'll give me a callback number we can talk. Thanks."

"Hmmm, I'm probably too early. I'll read the *Seattle Times* sports page, catch up on the Nationals, and call back in thirty minutes."

* * *

This time the call went through.

"Hi, Abdul. You don't know me …. Yeah, it's okay that we speak in Farsi—but I know something about you …. Yes, of course I'm an American, but I have long-ago roots in Iran. I'm visiting from the DC area, and I'd like to meet you. I've something to share that should be appealing …. I promise. It won't take long, maybe fifteen, twenty minutes …. Okay, I'll come to your home. I have your address and a rental car."

Abdul's home address was listed as 2405 – 84th Avenue, Clyde Hill. That meant the man could afford to live in an expensive neighborhood, which wasn't surprising considering that he was a highly paid Microsoft computer guy. Jeff's GPS found the address easily, and he parked in front of the three-car garage, walked a few steps to the front door, and rang the doorbell.

The door opened. "As-salaam 'alaykum!"

"Alaykum as-salaam!"

"Come in, come in. You should know that my curiosity is killing me. Here, have a seat."

"Thanks, Abdul. You look just like your pictures, and I've seen a few of those."

"You don't say. How so?"

"Sure, I'll get to the point. I'm Jeff Khavari. I'm from the CIA and my office probably knows more about you than you'd like, but that's the way we do things."

"Yeah, well to be honest about it, I'm not surprised. How many guys do you think would call me and out of the blue start jabbering away in Farsi?"

"True, for sure. By the way, are we alone? Can we talk freely?"

"Not to worry. I'm divorced, as you no doubt know, but I do have a lady friend who occasionally spends the night here. That's the reason for the three-car garage. One space for her, one for me, and the third for our two-seat OVR and trailer which we occasionally drive up into the Cascades. She's an outdoors freak, and I love her the more for it. But right now she's on a shopping spree across the lake in Seattle, so we have plenty of time."

"Hmmm. How serious is this, Abdul? Are you two thinking about a wedding?"

"That's a real possibility. She's a live wire, and she's adding a lot of zip to my life."

"What's her name?"

"Suzy. Actually, it's Suzanne Weatherby. He father has made millions in real estate, here on the East Side. And if you're thinking about her being involved with you CIA spooks, you'll need to get her a clearance."

"Let's not get ahead of ourselves, Abdul. You need to know why we're talking because you might not like what you're about to hear."

"Try me."

"Okay. Here's the deal. You may not know it yet, but the CIA has an enormous database. We've been collecting names from all over the world for more than seventy years. And included in that database are the names of your grandparents, Habib and Leila Nazari."

"Yeah, I remember my folks talking about them. They got out just in time, before the mullahs took over in 1979. My granddad made a small fortune by investing in the Anglo-Iranian Oil Company, before it was nationalized by that commie creep Mohammad Mosaddeq. Fortunately, they made it to Paris and eventually became French citizens and that's where the two of them are buried, in a cemetery reserved for French Muslims."

"Speaking of which, how goes it with your faith? You're Muslim, I assume."

"Frankly, I'm Muslim in name only. When I was much younger, my folks made me memorize the Qur'an, which I did, nearly all of it. And they dragged me to Friday worship services at that mosque in South Seattle. But I've given a lot of thought to Muhammad's claims, and now I don't believe a word of what he said. Besides, Suzy is a Christian, and I've been going to church with her."

"Hmmm. Well, those details are new to me, but they'll give you something to talk about if you accept my proposal."

"Which is?"

"Okay, before I get to that, we need to know a little more about your intended, Suzanne Weatherby. You mentioned a security clearance, and to get that I need her date and place of birth, her parents' names, any siblings, current employer, that sort of stuff."

"Sure. She was born in Seattle on March 21, 1998. We joke about that, actually. I call her a *No Rooz* baby, with March 21 being the first day of the Persian new year, as you should know.

"And you should know something about Suzy's job. She's an RN at Children's Hospital, out there near Magnuson Park; got her degree at the U-Dub School of Nursing. She loves kids and says that after we get married, she wants to have at least two of her own!

"You should also know that Suzy's mom is half Persian, third generation from before the 1979 revolution. That's why she speaks passable Farsi. And she's getting better at it. I encourage her, and we talk to each other in Farsi every morning while we're eating breakfast.

"Okay, so much for the personal stuff. I'm listening. Tell me more."

"I mentioned the CIA's enormous database. Well, we've searched that database with a microscope, and believe it or not, *your* name popped up as the one we were looking for. In other words, my people at headquarters believe you're uniquely qualified for the job we have in mind. 'What kind of job?' you ask."

"Of course."

"This will be tricky, Abdul, and I'll be up front with you about that. We intend to integrate you into a branch of the Red

Crescent, likely the Lebanese branch, because our station in Beirut has a solid contact with the local Red Crescent leader. And now that we know that Suzy's mother is Persian and Suzy knows Farsi, it should be possible for the two of you to go over there as a team."

"With what purpose?"

"Ostensibly, to offer specialized help to those who need it, especially kids, now that we know about Suzy's work at Children's. This Red Crescent thing, we believe, is very good cover because it will give you access to all kinds of people. The organization has an office in Tehran, and we're hoping that when it gets word from Beirut about you and Suzy, you'll be a welcome addition to the group's staff. There are only four of them, working out of a small office in downtown Tehran."

"Look, Jeff, if I accept your deal—and I won't do it without talking to Suzy—I'll be at some risk, no matter how good this Red Crescent cover might be. I won't have diplomatic immunity, like most of you CIA guys have, so if I'm caught with my pants down, I'm in deep doo-doo. The same for Suzy, only worse because she's a woman. Assuming she goes along with this, what would your people say to buying us a ten million dollar life insurance policy, with Suzy's and my folks as the beneficiaries?"

"Hmmm. That sounds reasonable to me, but that kind of decision is way above my pay grade. Tell you what, as soon as I get back to headquarters, I'll report all this to my superiors, and we should have an answer within forty-eight hours. I have your phone number, and I'll let you know."

Three

Friday, July 6, 2018, 1400 hours, at the Imam Shirazi mosque in central Tehran. The worshippers are departing, most of them on foot.

"What a beautiful service, don't you think?"

"Indeed, I agree. Although imam Jabbar has been with us for only two months, he certainly knows how to deliver a message. Allah, peace be upon him, would be proud."

"What I liked most about the service today: Nobody stared at me or asked questions."

"That's not surprising, considering all the gossip that's been floating throughout our congregation, about your special relationship. Everybody—now—knows that you're our supreme leader's granddaughter. After last week's flare-up, they know they're expected to treat you just like anyone else. And that's easier said than done, considering you're one of the most beautiful women in Tehran."

"Yes, that's such a relief. I feel as though I can pretend to be just like anyone. And it's so good to have a close friend, someone in whom I can confide when I'm not sure what to do next."

"And that would be?"

"Esfir Sohrab. She and I grew up together, from first grade on. We were very close, and we still are. She and I talk to each other at least once a week."

"How's it going with Hussein?"

"Oh, I don't know. He's such a bother. That trip to Europe was his downfall."

"How so?"

"He was only eighteen at the time. The trip was a high school graduation present from our parents. He spent a few days in Paris, hanging out with some other Persian teens, and he learned to drink. Wine at first, then the harder stuff. I think now he's a closet alcoholic. He won't admit it, but I'm pretty sure that's true. And he's so well known here in Tehran it's hard for him to find a place to drink without people learning about it. Worse, probably, he can't hold a job. His wife divorced him last year; it's just awful."

"How does he feel about you?"

"He resents me, and he doesn't care that I know it. I tried to love him when he was little, but not anymore. Nowadays we hardly ever speak, even though we have each other's phone numbers."

"Are your reservations in order? You said you're leaving Tuesday."

"Finally, yes. I have a first class seat on Iran Air's Airbus A320, nonstop, Tehran to Beirut and back. Good for one week. I got the ticket online and used a fake name. Grandpa arranged that for me. It's a credit card in another name, and it lets me buy stuff without giving away my true identity. The same with my hotel reservation in Beirut, at the Four Seasons. I'm on the fourth floor with a beautiful view of the ocean. And the room is suitable for two persons. Mustafa knows I'm coming, and he'll want to spend some time with me. In fact, he might even propose marriage; wouldn't surprise me if he did."

"That could be dangerous, Roya, if anyone should find out."

"You know, cousin, I really don't care anymore. I'm twenty-five years old—that's old enough to live my own life. I'm sick and tired of having to pretend I'm somebody I'm not."

"Okay if I drive you to the airport?"

"Absolutely. You're the best friend I have here."

* * *

It was tough but Mustafa finally decided it was the right thing to do. The day before he'd asked his boss if he could have the next morning to himself; "Some business to take care of," he lied. And he didn't have much time. She would be checking into the hotel the next afternoon, and she'd expect him to call within the hour.

* * *

"American Embassy, how may I direct your call?"

"Uh, you don't know me, but I have something to discuss with your intelligence people. I can't talk about it on the phone but it's important enough that I come to your embassy. Can you get me an appointment, say tomorrow morning between nine and eleven?"

"One moment please, I'll check. —Yes, we'll expect you a little after nine. When you get here, you'll have to sign in with the Marine guard.

"—Mr. Matthews, this is Sergeant Davis at the front desk. I just got a call from a guy who says he wants to talk to someone in our intelligence office. That would be you, of course. He sounded like he's Lebanese, perfect Arabic, but I sensed he really does have something important to say. He'll be here a little after nine."

"Thanks, Sergeant. I'll be ready."

* * *

Tony Matthews was into his second year as the CIA's Chief of Station in Beirut. He'd made a direct transfer from Baghdad, and the Beirut assignment was a reward for work well done with the Iraqi intelligence service. He knew all about walk-ins, of course; that was SOP from his years-ago training, but he'd never actually met one. So he was naturally curious about this man that Sergeant Davis had just told him about. All he knew was that he was likely a Lebanese national who spoke perfect Arabic. Not much to go on; he'd have to wait. Sergeant Davis would escort the man to the embassy's waiting room, and they could talk there.

* * *

The next morning at 0910.

"I'm the guy you talked to yesterday. My name is Mustafa Shadid, and you asked me to be here around nine o'clock. So what happens now?"

"Okay, Mustafa, if you'll step over there and into that waiting room I'll call the man you're looking for. Shouldn't be more than a couple of minutes.

"—Sergeant Davis here. His name is Mustafa and he's waiting."

* * *

"Good morning, Mustafa. Welcome to a little bit of the United States. You say you want to talk to an American intelligence officer, and that's what I am. You don't need to know my name, not yet, anyway. So please, tell me why you're here."

"Yeah, I suppose I'd be rude to ask you for some ID, but I'll take your word for it. And I doubt that what I'm about to tell you will make much sense. No way to check it for facts; you'll just have to take my word for it."

"That's fair enough. Go ahead."

"Okay. Here's my story. And by the way, I assume you have a recording device running somewhere, and that's good because you won't have to remember everything I'm about to tell you.

"My name is Mustafa Shadid. I have a degree in nursing from the American University, here in Beirut. Right now, I'm interning at a clinic in suburban Beirut, the Mercy House. It's mainly a home for orphaned children. That's something you can verify with one phone call.

"And here's something else you can check out to prove that I'm telling the truth. You call the Four Seasons hotel and ask if they have a reservation for a woman whose name is Roya Khamenei."

"What—who?"

"One and the same. Ayatollah Khamenei's granddaughter. She's not what you could call a princess, but pretty close to it.

"And this is the good part. She and I are in love, and she expects me to ask her to marry me, probably in the next day or two."

John Sager

"Whoa, Mustafa, why are you telling me this?"

"Because I have absolutely no love for what her granddaddy is doing. Iran is a mess, and the whole world knows it. And over the next few days I'm going to talk to her about how *she* feels. I intend to remind her that when the old man dies—what, he's nearly 80, and that exceeds the life expectancy for most Persians—she's going to be just like any other Persian. Sure, she'll probably have a healthy inheritance, but what's she going to do with it? You can only buy so many Persian rugs! I intend to try to persuade her that when he does die, she and I can live here, in Beirut. I can teach her to speak Arabic. She's smart, she's only twenty-five, and if she agrees, she'll have the whole world in front of her.

"And not so incidentally, she is one beautiful woman. If she wanted to, she could make a living by doing photos for *Paris Match*."

"Okay, Mustafa. I assume you're telling me this because you'd like to help us. For example, I can picture you going to Tehran with Roya, taking a look for yourself, and reporting back. To be honest, we don't have many assets in Iran, and she likely has some valuable insights about what the leadership *really* thinks, its plans for the future, names of important officials, that sort of thing.

"Before you leave, I'd like to photocopy your Lebanese ID card and passport. That should tell me enough about you that I can report to my headquarters in Washington. We need to ask for what we call a security clearance, and once that's in hand, then we're good to go.

"One more thing, Mustafa. I already like you, and I'm willing to trust you. My name is Tony Matthews, and if there's anything I can do for you, I'm just a phone call away."

Four

Monday, July 9, 2018, 0930 hours, CIA Headquarters,

in the office of Sam Wolters, Chief, Near East Division.

"Hey, Tom, Have you seen this cable from Beirut? Came in overnight."

"Just read it, Sam. Looks like good news."

"I should say so. Give credit where it's due. Tony Matthews has done it again, persuading that man to join his team. And even though he's a walk-in, it took a lot of guts for him to agree to Tony's proposal. If he were ever found out to be helping the CIA, even the ayatollah's granddaughter couldn't help him."

"I checked our registry about an hour ago, and sure enough, we have a file on the Khamenei clan, including the granddaughter. And she really is a beauty—long black hair, brown eyes but without that too-big nose that bedevil so many Persian women."

"Do you think that when push comes to shove she'll be willing to do her new husband's bidding? In Tehran she'd be considered a traitor, notwithstanding her family connections."

"Who knows? We have to rely on her husband to make this work. And as long as Tony Matthews is in the loop, I'm not going to worry about it."

* * *

"Okay, Tom, we have another matter to deal with. I believe you've read the ops proposal from Jeff Khavari. He prepared it as soon as he returned from his trip to Bellevue.

"Just finished this morning. And as we speak, I'm running traces on these two. Assuming they're clean, we'll have their security clearances within forty-eight hours. But it'll be a real challenge, getting this couple integrated with our Red Crescent friends. It's perfect cover, providing your doctor-friend agrees."

"Yeah, I've already given him a heads-up about this. He reminded me of something I should have remembered. The Red Crescent office in Tehran is down to four people, so adding this new couple should be helpful. The fact that both of them speak Farsi will help. Our biggest problem, of course, is to try to pass them off as Canadian citizens. Our Technical Services Division will provide them with fabricated Canadian passports and ID cards, and that will be enough to get them through passport control at Mehrabad airport."

"I've been thinking about this. Maybe we should connect with the Canadians, just to be safe."

"You're probably right about that but we need to remember that our president is insisting that there be *no American fingerprints*—his words—linked to his regime-change idea."

"Look, it was the president who gave director Franklin that order. Why can't we ask him to contact the Canadians? We can't expect this Nazari couple to go out there completely naked, without any kind of backup. I think the director should do whatever it takes to get word to the Canadian embassy in Tehran. They don't need to know about the regime-change angle, only that this couple is going out there to help the local Red Crescent office. It's strictly a humanitarian thing, nothing to do with espionage."

* * *

Two days later, in Director Franklin's office.

"Sally, I need to talk to Sir Peter Mackenzie. He's the head of the Canadian intelligence service; his office is in Ottawa. Is it possible for me to talk to him over our secure line?"

"I believe it is. Let me check, I'll get back to you in a couple of minutes. —Yes, Mr. Mackenzie is on the line."

"Peter, this is David Franklin. You'll remember me from that conference in Washington last year."

"Yes, I do remember. What can I do for you?"

"Good. Peter, we're sending a couple to Tehran. They're to be documented as Canadian citizens because, as you know, the mullahs would never allow an American to set foot there. Their names are Abdul and Suzanne Nazari, from Bellevue, Washington, and they've agreed to undertake this mission."

"To what purpose?"

"They'll be integrated into the local Red Crescent office. They've had a lot of experience with helping families, especially kids, and they'll be doing interviews and offering help where it's needed. The purpose is to collect anecdotal evidence about how typical families see themselves now that the mullahs have been running the country for forty years. We intend to use the information as a psych war weapon, when and if the opportunity arises."

"And I presume you want me to tell our embassy in Tehran about this?"

"Exactly so. They'll want to have a place to go, to be among English-speaking friends, pick up their mail, recharge their batteries."

"What's the security level for this?"

"As high as we can make it. Without diplomatic immunity, these two would be in big trouble if their cover is blown."

"Okay, David. I'll see that it happens. And good luck!"

Franklin hangs up and says to himself: "Good. The old boy network is alive and well."

Five

"*You what?* You told him we're willing to pack up and leave everything, go to Washington, DC, and then to Tehran? As Canadian citizens? You must be crazy! What in the world were you thinking?"

"Hey, hey, sweetheart, easy does it. Of course I told him I wouldn't agree to anything without your approval. If you'd been here, you would have seen what a nice guy he is and how much sense he made."

"Okay, run this by me one more time, slowly."

"Sure. The first thing you need to understand is that this is not just some CIA pipe dream. This *program*, if that's what we want to call it, comes directly from the White House, no kidding. President Oglethorpe wants this to happen, and it turns out that, after a lot of searching, the CIA has decided that you and I are as well suited as anyone to help make it happen."

"Wait a minute. You say 'help' make it happen. Are there others?"

"Yes, absolutely. You and I, if we agree to do this, will not be alone. I don't know who the others will be, not yet, anyway, but I was assured that there will be others."

"So what about *us*, you and me? We've been planning to get married. Is that still likely?"

"It certainly is. They *want* us to do this as a team. I told them about your work at Children's, and that fits perfectly. You'll be doing the same thing over there, working with kids who need help. The only difference is that you'll be speaking to one another in Farsi."

"Why Canadian? What's that got to do with anything?"

"Because the Iranians would never allow two Americans to set foot on their turf. Not even for a humanitarian cause; that's how spooked they are. But Canada, even though it's right next door, the Iranians don't much care about that."

"Is there a time limit on this thing? How long do they expect us to stay over there?"

"I don't think anyone knows. Until we get the job done, I suppose."

"Meaning what? 'Getting the job done'?"

"Sweetheart, what it means is *regime change*. When the Iranian people decide they've had enough of the ayatollahs and the mullahs, they'll insist on something better. It'll be their choice, of course, but it won't be another theocracy, like they have now."

"So just how do we contribute to this program? Heck, we're only two people."

"Like Mr. Khavari said, you build a wall one brick at a time. We won't be the only ones working this problem. It's not for us to know how this will happen; that's up to the experts in Washington."

"Okay, another question. What does one do for *fun* in Tehran? It sounds like a terribly dull place, with all the restrictions, especially for women."

"Glad you asked; I've done a little research. Within a ten-minute drive north, you're into some of the most imposing mountains on planet Earth. They're called the Elburz and Mt. Tochal, which you can practically reach out and touch, is a ten-thousand-foot peak. Plenty of snow in winter for skiing and snowboarding, and plenty of trails for our ORV in the other months."

"What happens if we're found out? A firing squad, prison, what?"

"Probably none of the above. The Iranians are on pretty good terms with the Canadians, and I doubt they'd want to poison the well. They'd likely ask us go home and leave it at that. But in the worst case scenario, Mr. Khavari promised that the Agency will buy a ten-million-dollar life insurance policy for us, with our parents as beneficiaries."

"Have you prayed about this?"

"I have, and I believe God approves. But until now I haven't said anything to you."

"Well, okay, sweetheart. You've twisted my arm, but gently. So yes, you can tell Mr. Khavari that I'm on board."

Six

It was a little after midnight, and something told Hussein he should be heading for home and a good night's sleep. That something was his conscience, and he understood that, if barely. His immediate problem was finding a place that was still open. Finally, he spotted a taxi, hailed its driver, and slid into the backseat.

"Jordan's Place, and step on it!"

"Hey, man, you got enough money to pay for the trip? It's about ten kilometers."

"If you knew who I am, you wouldn't ask such a stupid question."

"Oh, is that so. Just who are you, anyway. One of the royals?"

"Matter of fact, that's exactly who I am. How come you're so smart?"

"Yeah, I'll believe that when the sun rises in the west."

"Here, goofball, look at my ID."

"Well, I'll be. You're the old man's grandson. I didn't mean to be rude—sorry about that."

"No problem. Just get me there before the place closes."

"I believe it's open all night. The cops are on the take, as you probably know. It's the only place in the city where you can drink and get away with it. And the women who hang around … some of them are for sale, I've been told."

"Yeah, yeah, I know all that. That's why I want to get there before it closes. I have a lady friend who's expecting me. They have rooms on the second floor, and we'll probably spend the night there."

Even though he was half-drunk, Hussein hoped this fairy tale was believable. But he really did need another drink, and he might find a young woman who would agree to use one of those upstairs rooms.

* * *

Ten minutes and 100,000 rials later, the cab dropped off its inebriated patron. Hussein staggered through the open entry gate and into one of the larger lounges. From there he could see most of what he wanted to see. But first, another shot of on-the-rocks Jack Daniels, imported from oh-so-friendly Lebanon.

* * *

Much earlier, before Hussein became addicted, he had heard
about this Jordan's Place. It was named after Samuel Jordan, a
Presbyterian missionary and founder of the American College
of Tehran, which eventually closed its doors in 1941. Later,
its location on Nelson Mandela Boulevard came to be known
simply as Jordan's Place, and over the years the neighborhood
morphed into one of the most expensive residential areas in
the city. Wealthy Persians flocked to the neighborhood, there
to patronize its upscale restaurants, boutiques, and markets.

But now Hussein was hooked on alcohol and drugs, and he hadn't
held a job in two years. Fortunately for him, the Khamenei estate
planners had assured him a lifetime pension, which he routinely
drew on from Iran's central bank. And like everyone else, it
bugged Hussein no end that the rial was virtually worthless on
the international currency exchange. Last time he checked an
American one-cent piece was buying 425 rials.

Most if not all of Tehran's elite knew that Jordan's Place had
become *the* venue for Tehran's twenty-to-thirty-somethings, a

hangout for the young, spoiled, and affluent men and women who long since had abandoned their Muslim faith and Muslim ways. Liquor was easily available, as were some of the young women who patronized Jordan's Place. He understood that management frowned on the presence of prostitutes, something the local police felt obliged to prevent, but meeting a woman of that persuasion and then taking her home later in the night— perfectly okay.

But Hussein's *real* reason for coming to this sin palace was to chat with one of the bartenders, a man he had come to know from earlier visits. The man's name was Ali Kazemi, and his brother, Mustafa Kazemi, was a VAJA officer, assigned to the Royal Palace in downtown Tehran.

Hussein walked up to the bar, got Ali's attention, and asked if he had a few moments to talk.

"What's up, friend? You look like you've already had one too many."

"Not quite, Ali. And you probably know why I'm here. What's the latest on my dear, dear sister?"

"Oh, that again? Hey, you know I'm not supposed to talk about it. That's sort of classified information, in case you've forgotten."

"Bullshit. You're talking to the ayatollah's grandson, and you tell him whatever he wants to know."

"Yeah, I know that. Okay, here's the latest. Your sister, as we speak, is in Beirut. She's staying at the Four Seasons hotel, and we believe she's seeing her boyfriend, a Lebanese guy name of Mustafa Shadid. Our source believes these two are pretty tight, possibly intending to marry. Her reservation is for four days, after which she's to return to Tehran. When that happens, you can ask her yourself, what she's up to."

"Not likely. That bitch and I haven't spoken to each other for years. And if I were to get close enough to speak to her, I'd probably strangle her. So no, but thanks for the info.

"By the way, is Fatima here tonight?"

"She is, she's in my office, updating our menu. She expects you to take her home tonight."

"Yeah, she's a great lay, and she knows it. I'm pretty sure she wants to marry me, and who wouldn't? Heck, she'd become part of the royal family. But it ain't gonna happen.

"Now, I'd like another drink, if you don't mind."

Seven

The next day Hussein slept off his hangover until nearly noon, got up, relieved himself, and reached for the Tylenol bottle. Three tablets would get him through the next several hours, and he had an important decision to make. Should he tell his father what he had learned about Roya? As he saw it, Roya had been spoiled rotten by her parents *and* her grandfather, the ayatollah. Some of her classmates thought of her as the *poor little rich girl*, but no one ever dared say so aloud. Privately, however, Hussein admitted to himself that she had behaved like her peers, she never spoke of her royal heritage, she dressed modestly, and she was a friend to anyone who bothered to get to know her.

And she was smart, curious and determined to learn whatever she could about the outside world. For example: The day following Ruhollah Khomeini's ascension to power, following the 1979 revolution, he told his new nation's parliament what he thought of the United States: *America is the Great Satan, the Wounded Snake.* That quotation had become a mantra for Iran's politicians, and nearly forty years later, Iran's citizens were expected to respond accordingly to anything American. But before she had entered high school, Roya Khamenei let it be known that she didn't believe a word of it.

As a teen, she managed to acquire an iPhone, and she used it primarily to stay abreast of what was happening in Europe and the United States. Although the scripts were translated into Farsi, she decided to study English and found that Tehran's school system didn't offer that language—*The Great Satan* problem. So she found an online classroom, emanating from somewhere in Israel, that offered spoken English language lessons five days each week, one hour at a time.

Hussein's problem, he admitted, was that to everyone but himself, his sister was a rather remarkable women, even at the tender age of twenty-five years. Still, he believed it was his duty to tell their father what he had learned about his little sister.

* * *

At 10:00 a.m. the next day.

"You called and said you wanted to talk. Frankly, I'm surprised you're *able* to talk, what with the way you've been behaving lately. Be very careful, Hussein, lest you bring shame to this family. For all I know, people are already beginning to talk. I know you've been visiting Jordan's Place, and probably many others know.

"But you didn't come here to be scolded. So tell me, why are you here?"

"Thank you, Father. Yes, you're right, as usual. But what I have to say is very much worth your hearing, when you mention bringing shame on our family."

"And how might that be?"

"It's about Roya, your daughter, my sister. I learned this only yesterday while I was at Jordan's Place. And I learned this from someone you know and trust, although I'd rather not reveal his name. Let's say he's an important part of the palace entourage."

"Hmm. All right, I'm listening."

"Roya, right now, is in Beirut. She's there to meet a man she intends to marry. He's a Lebanese citizen, and probably an Arab, although I'm not certain about that. His name is Mustafa Shadid. My guess is that after they're married, she'll stay with him in Beirut, although that's only a guess. If they were to return to Tehran, I should think she'd find it difficult to explain everything to her friends.

"And apparently, she's said nothing to you about this. Since when does a young Persian woman not have to tell her father about her intention to marry?"

"You should know the answer to that question as well as I, Hussein. Roya is, what, twenty-five? She considers herself part of the new generation. She follows events in America and Europe, like most of her friends do, and she considers our ways old-fashioned and far too restrictive. I'd guess that most of the young people who patronize Jordan's Place feel the same way.

"And she's well aware that you don't approve of her. You should know, Hussein, that is something that weighs heavily on your mother's heart; mine, too, I should add."

"Yes, I understand that. But what do you intend to do about it? I'm part of this family too, and I'm just as concerned as you are about Roya's bringing shame to our name!"

"Someday, Hussein, should you become a legitimate father, you'll see things differently. To answer your question, I don't intend to do *anything* about this. I read a novel recently about life in America. According to its author, they have a saying which grew out of their Civil War: 'I'm free, white and twenty-one, and I'll do as I please.'

"Roya is old enough to make her own decisions. We might not approve of them, but there's nothing we can or should do about that. And please, Hussein, when she does return, with or without a husband, try to treat her as you would like to be treated. You would have no reason to know it, but in some cultures this is known as the Golden Rule."

Eight

French Embassy, Tehran, Tuesday, July 10, 2018.

"And what is the purpose of your visit to Paris, Mr. Safavi?"

"My grandmother lives there. She's invited me to come for a visit. And it should be cooler there than it is here. My thermometer read thirty-nine degrees yesterday afternoon. Here's the letter she wrote; I received it last week."

"I see. Very well, this is our standard visitor's visa; it's good for two weeks. You'll need to show your Iranian passport when you arrive at the Paris Orly airport. And when you return to

Tehran, you should surrender this visa to your immigration officials.

"Have a good trip."

* * *

Abdullah Safavi's grandmother Sanaz was one of the lucky ones, able to leave Tehran the day before Ruhollah Khomeini returned to Tehran and declared himself Supreme Leader of the new Islamic Republic of Iran. She had purchased a one-way ticket, nonstop Tehran to Paris, two weeks earlier, and her reserved seat was one of only three still available on the Air France flight. Only twenty-six years old at the time, she had heard the warning signals along with a few friends, listening to Voice of America reports about the impending regime change. She had heard about the Iranian expatriate community in and around Paris and decided she could make a new life for herself in that environment.

Abdullah's mother had not been so fortunate. She was one of a large group of women who participated in the early downtown street demonstrations against the new regime. She was arrested and accused of treason; then she was tried in a sharia court and sentenced to ten years in Tehran's infamous Evin Prison. She had been there less than a week when she was raped by one of the prison guards. The next day she slashed her wrists and bled to death.

It was his mother's death that motivated her son to make the journey to Paris.

* * *

American Embassy, Paris. CIA Chief of Station Dennis Atwood has just finished speaking with his deputy, Chris Mayberry.

"She told you her grandson is coming to visit?"

"Indeed. And she added that he's on the short list of new candidates for hire by their intel service, VAJA. He's been working for their foreign ministry but has never been given an overseas assignment, and he thought this switch might make a difference."

"And if memory serves, at your previous meeting she told you she intends to have a serious talk with him about Islam."

"That's what she said. She converted to Catholicism a couple of years after coming to Paris and has concluded that Islam has no future. And she worries about that. The woman has scads of friends in Iran, and she fears the mullahs and ayatollahs are destroying the country. She sees her grandson as a guy who might be able to slow this down—maybe, someday, with a lot of help, put a stop to it."

"I presume you'll see her again, after she's spent some time with her grandson?"

"She'll call me the moment he leaves. And I'd love to be that mouse in her pocket when the two chat."

"Would she be willing to wear a wire?"

"We need to remember, Dennis, that Sanaz Safavi is seventy-five years old. She was only ten when Muhammad Mosaddeq came on the scene, and she remembers what a disaster that was. At that age she was only vaguely aware of what *Tudeh* meant, the Farsi equivalent of *Communist*, but she certainly remembers the havoc that Mosaddeq brought with him. He nationalized the Anglo-Iranian Oil Company, sent most of the British oilmen packing and then saw Iran's petroleum product plummet. That ill-advised move in itself caused a severe economic downturn, and within a year or so, many Iranians—especially those in the larger cities—were on the streets, begging for handouts.

"After a year or so of Mosaddeq's bumbling, the locals tired of it and staged their own coup d'état, for which, as you know, the CIA was blamed as the instigator. Of course, we know better. It really was an internal uprising, with the Agency providing moral support, telling the leaders that if they were successful, they would have the full backing of the United States government.

"During her teen years, Sanaz became something of a personality in her own right. She was smart, good looking, popular with her peers. She told me that at one time she believed that the shah, Reza Pahlavi, was the world's handsomest man. She became enamored with the royal family, and when the shah was forced to leave, she was absolutely crushed. Even today she considers herself a 'royalist,' and is not ashamed to say so.

"So no, I don't believe we should ask her to wear a wire. If she were to do that, she'd feel like a real spy, and she's not ready for that, not yet."

* * *

Abdullah's Air France flight 755 departed Mehrabad airport at 0900 and arrived at Orly three and a half hours later. He used that time to think about the possibilities. Five years ago, he had been accepted as a candidate-officer in Iran's Ministry of Foreign Affairs, but he had yet to receive an overseas assignment. Then without telling anyone, he applied for an appointment to VAJA, Iran's intelligence agency, believing that such an assignment was likely to result in some kind of overseas duty.

Two days before leaving for Paris he was told that he was on a short list and probably would receive an appointment within the next thirty days. This was very good news because it meant that he could somehow, someday, seek the vengeance he wanted for his mother's horrible death, a death decreed by an unelected, virtually unknown mullah who had presided over the verdict that sent her to prison. This would be uppermost in his mind when he visited his grandmother, Sanaz.

Another idea that he couldn't seem to shake: Did he really want to devote his life to supporting the ayatollahs and the mullahs? He had already seen enough evidence of their cruelty and capricious decisions, all of which appeared to be means by which to retain their hold on power. The aspirations of the average Iranian meant nothing to the country's leaders. Oh, sure, there was a supposedly democratically elected *majlis* that claimed to represent the people's wishes. But everyone knew the truth: It was the mullahs and, especially, Ayatollah Khamenei who made the decisions that mattered most.

And then there were the numerous occasions when he had visited Tehran's fast-food joints, Javid's Jungle his favorite. He preferred Javid's to the others because it had a reliable Wi-Fi hot spot, and he could sit for an hour, over several cups of tea, and catch up on what was happening in the "other world," as he liked to think of anyplace other than Iran. Although the authorities tried to jam those out-of-country frequencies, Javid had taught himself how to get around that, a secret he shared with his favorite customers. The system worked with

Abdullah's iPhone, and he typically used ten or fifteen minutes of his data plan to learn about political happenings in America, particularly Washington, DC. Only recently he had learned of the American president's decision to deny Iran's banking system access to all foreign exchange outlets. And that, he knew, had led to the rial's freefall on the world's market exchanges.

He felt himself coming closer and closer to the decision he knew he should make: try to do *something* to bring his country back to normalcy. But what could one man do about all this? He hoped his grandmother would have something to say about that.

Nine

Abdullah's cab took him directly to his grandmother's home. She had written that she no longer felt safe driving her own car in Paris; so she had sold it and was now relying on the city's superb metro system, on those few occasions when she left her neighborhood. Abdullah's first challenge: How to converse with his cabdriver, neither of whom knew the other's language? A carefully handwritten note with her address solved that problem, and after a forty-five-minute drive and a ninety-euro fare, he arrived, tired but satisfied. The two chatted away for nearly thirty minutes until Abdullah pleaded exhaustion. He found his way to the guest bedroom and was sound asleep in minutes.

* * *

Twenty-four hours later, Abdullah sat on the edge of his bed and reviewed his day. He had used his Olympus digital voice recorder—purchased for twenty-one million rials at a black market counter in Tehran's Grand Bazaar—to record their conversations, make notes, and prepare questions for tomorrow. He was most interested in what his grandmother had told him about her *new life in Jesus Christ,* as she had put it.

"What do you mean, Grammy?"

"Sweetheart, within two months of my arrival in Paris, I found two other families, expatriates from Tehran, one of whom I had known slightly because we had gone to the same mosque together. Noor Fawazi told me that she and her husband were going to a Catholic church, they had learned the mass rituals and had accepted Jesus as their Lord and Savior. It was a dangerous decision, as you know, because according to Iran's sharia law, a conversion to another faith is punishable by death. So they don't talk about it because they don't want anyone back home to learn about it."

"Why would they do such a thing, knowing what might happen if they're found out?"

"I'll tell you why. We've talked about this at great length, and that's why I, too, have become a Catholic. I go to mass with Noor and her husband every Sunday morning, and every Wednesday evening our church has a Bible study program. For about six weeks now, we've been learning about the differences between Christianity and Islam, and this is something I want you to understand too. It will change your life, sweetheart, trust me."

"Okay, Grammy, I'm listening."

"Good. The first thing I should say is that Christianity had been accepted throughout Europe for some 600 years *before* Muhammad appeared in Mecca. Muhammad claimed that Allah had spoken to him in visions and instructed him to write down his revelations in a book. But Muhammad was illiterate, so he told his friends about these revelations, and it was his friends who actually put the Qur'an to paper.

"You need to understand, sweetheart, that my Christian faith and the faith of every other Christian—and there are more than *two billion* of us—absolutely depends on these truths: One, that Jesus Christ was God's Son; two, that He was crucified by the Romans; and three, that He rose from the dead and ascended into heaven.

"And Muslims are expected to believe that everything they read in the Qur'an is absolute truth, spoken by Allah himself.

"Well, let's see about that. We're both wise enough to want to know what's true and what isn't. One thing the Qur'an claims is that it would be impossible for Allah to have a son. Muhammad's writings would have us believe that Allah was too majestic to have had a son; that he would have needed a wife, a wife whom he'd have to impregnate—but all of this is beneath Allah's character because, according to Muhammad, when Allah wants something, all he has to do is say, 'Be!' and it is. In other words, it is impossible to think of Jesus as God's son."

"Hmm, I've never thought of it that way, Grammy, but it's beginning to make sense."

"Good, you're a smart guy, and I can see that you're beginning to see the light. There's more, much more"

"I should think so. Go ahead."

"As I just said, my Christian faith depends on another truth: That Jesus was crucified. But the Qur'an specifically denies that He was crucified. The text claims that those of us who believe this are pursuing a conjecture, that there's nothing to it.

"And there's more, sweetheart. You've probably never heard of it but we Christians believe in something we call the Trinity. That means that God is mysteriously *three* persons: God, Jesus, and The Holy Spirit. There's plenty of evidence for this idea in the New Testament. But again, the Qur'an denies this and insists that this is impossible, that there is only one Allah. More than one, no."

"Granny, what about Muhammad as a *person*? I've studied the Qur'an and memorized most of it, but I see him as a powerful warrior and not much more than that."

"It's important that you know more than that, sweetheart. Muhammad began his ministry in Mecca when he was forty years old. He had a lot of trouble persuading the locals that what he was preaching was true because most of them were pagans, people who worshipped idols. However, his wife was an influential person, and that meant he was free to preach pretty much as he wished. However, after she died, he ran into fierce opposition, so much so that he decided to move north to the city of Medina.

"Scholars have been able to determine what parts of the Qur'an were written while Muhammad was in Mecca and those written after he moved to Medina. And we now understand that after he moved to Medina he became a different person. You said you remember him as a warrior, and that's what he became in Medina. He provoked a number of battles, he ordered the decapitation of his prisoners, and he broke his promises and decided he could have as many wives as he wanted."

"Not a very nice person, right?"

"Absolutely. I've decided he was a terrible person, and it really grieves me to know that so many Iranians, some of them dear friends, believe every word in that book."

"Well, Granny, what you've told me grieves me, too, because it's forcing me to change the way I think about Islam. Maybe I'll just wait awhile and see what happens."

"Here's a question for you, sweetheart. I'm certain that your supreme leader, Ali Khamenei, knows what I've just told you. After all, he's Iran's most famous scholar. If he knows what I've told you, what does that make him, in your judgment?"

"I suppose that makes him a hypocrite, a man who knows the truth but can't afford to admit it to anyone. And now that I think about it, that applies to everyone who works for him."

"And do you want to devote yourself to a career which helps keep Khamenei in power? Or would you consider doing something else?"

"Such as?"

"As you no doubt know, sweetheart, there many Iranians here in Paris—and elsewhere in Europe—who consider themselves *dissidents*. They—we—don't dare go out in the streets, carrying placards and using a bullhorn to demand changes back home. That would be dangerous, and it wouldn't accomplish anything.

But we do meet now and then, we talk about what we can do to resist what's going on Iran. And not too long ago, I met an American who shares our concerns and our interests. He's an official at the American embassy here in Paris. I'm sure he'd like to meet you."

"What kind of official?"

"He's an intelligence officer. He's never said so, but I'm sure he works for the CIA."

"Let's say I'm willing to meet this man. Should I trust him? Do *you?*"

"I certainly do. I've told him a few things about you. I would not have done that if I didn't trust him."

"Hmm. Okay, Granny, I'll meet your American friend but *only* if you're present and we do it right here in your home. No way am I going to be seen going into the American embassy.

Remember, I'm just an interview away from being accepted as an officer-candidate in VAJA, and if anyone should learn that I'm talking to an American intelligence officer—well, you can imagine what would happen. I believe the Americans have an expression for this: 'I'd be toast.'"

* * *

Seventy-two hours later, American Embassy, Paris. Chris Mayberry is about to debrief himself.

"So, Chris, how'd it go?"

"You know, Dennis, that woman is remarkable. It would be fair to say that she had already persuaded her grandson to sign up with us. I suppose I'll get credit for recruiting the guy, but it was really her doing."

"How far were you able to go with him?"

"He accepted the commo plan without batting an eye. I gave him the modified iPhone, showed him how to use it. That took less than a couple of minutes. He's one smart dude, and I'm virtually certain that he'll be accepted by VAJA after he gets home."

"What about the EEIs? Did he buy those?"

"Not a problem. He probably could have written them himself."

"What about the woman, his grandmother."

"We absolutely have to trust her, Dennis. He insisted that she be there during the entire conversation. So she knows as much as he does. But, and this is important, it was obvious to me that these two are very close. He probably envies her freedom as a French citizen, and someday he'll probably want to join her."

"Did the faith thing come up?"

"Oh, yes, it certainly did. After talking to his grandmother, he has some serious misgivings about Islam, especially the way the sharia courts work in Tehran. And that's the key to his motivation. Something we couldn't have anticipated, but his mother was tried in a sharia court—she'd been arrested for participating with other women in a protest march in downtown Tehran—and found guilty of treason. The judge sent her off to Tehran's Evin Prison, and we know what a hellhole that place is. Ten years, he said. Sure enough, within a few days she was raped by one of the goon-guards, and the next day she slashed her wrists and bled to death.

"And that's what motivated her son, our new asset, to come to Paris."

"Okay, Chris. Good job. Write it up for headquarters, and I'll sign off. I'm guessing this is one of the few—maybe the only—asset we have in Tehran. Langley will insist on keeping the lid on this thing, limiting the knowledge of it to only a handful of people.

Ten

Wednesday, August 1, 2018, 2330 hours, The Four Seasons Hotel, Beirut, room 403.

The two lovers lay there, side by side, silently staring at the ceiling. From the faint glow of a faraway streetlamp they could see the shadows of gently-swaying palm trees. Roya was the first to speak.

"That was absolutely perfect, Mustafa, and I love you the more for it. You could tell I'm a virgin, but you were so gentle and patient. How did you learn to make love like that?"

"Look, Roya, you have no reason to believe this but I'm a virgin myself. I've done some reading, of course, and talked with the guys I work with. Yes, I do believe we're going to be the perfect married couple. Let's get some sleep, and we can talk in the morning."

* * *

Before leaving Tehran, Roya had decided to keep things as simple and unobtrusive as possible. Although nearly everyone in Tehran recognized her as she walked down a street, that would be different in Beirut. She was quite certain that no one knew she was here, and anyone who saw her might recognize her as a Persian, but no more than that.

They stepped out of the shower, helped each other dry off, got dressed, and took the elevator to one of the hotel's coffee shops. Roya knew that her Farsi wouldn't help in an Arabic-speaking culture, but she noticed that the menu was printed in both Arabic and English.

"What do you recommend, sweetheart? I know nothing about Arab food."

"Doesn't have to be Arab, love. This place has American food, if you want to try it."

"Really? *Ham*, in an *Arab* coffee shop?"

"Like I said, this place caters to almost as many Americans as it does us locals. If you're thinking about something different, try their ham and eggs, with buttered toast and strawberry jam. And the coffee should be good too. Tell you what, I'll order the same thing for both of us; that'll make it easier for our waiter and the kitchen. And while we're waiting, let's have a look at the morning newspaper."

* * *

After breakfast, Mustafa suggested they walk the short distance to the beach. At eight thirty in the morning, the hotel's beach crew had finished setting up sun umbrellas and lounge chairs, and they found themselves alone. It was the moment Mustafa had hoped for—time for some serious talk with his beautiful Roya.

"Roya, you should know this is coming, but we need talk about getting married. You said last night that's what you want most, the main reason you came here from Tehran."

"Of course, Mustafa. You're the only man I've ever loved, and I know you feel the same way about me."

"So we should decide a few things about our wedding. Do you want to do it here or in Tehran? And who performs the wedding? Do you want an imam to do it, or would you prefer what we call a civil ceremony?"

"Yes, I've been thinking about that. We should definitely do it here, before I'm due to return. I believe that when we marry I become a Lebanese citizen. People at home will be aghast when they learn about this, but I really don't care. As to your question about the kind of ceremony, I definitely prefer what you call a civil ceremony. But I know nothing about how we might do this."

"Hmm. I've been thinking about that too, sweetheart. It's what you might call an audacious option, but we *could* be married, here in Beirut, by an *American* clergyman."

"Seriously? You're not kidding?"

"No, I'm not. Maybe you haven't heard of it, but there's a university here, the American University of Beirut; the students refer to it as AUB. It attracts young men and women from all over the Middle East. It's Christian in its perspective and has chapel services every evening. The professors teach in English and Arabic. And I happen to know one of them. We could have a quiet ceremony, and I can arrange to have two witnesses, one for each of us. Matter of fact, I'm thinking about a man I met only a few days ago. He's an officer at the American embassy. I'm sure he'd agree to be my witness."

"How about one for me?"

"Let's think about that for a minute. After we're married, we don't have to prove it to anyone. The marriage certificate is just a piece of paper that we might want to have when we have children; other than that, people will take our word for it. Plus, you'll be wearing a ring on your left hand.

"As for a witness, we could ask one of the ladies here at the hotel, or I could ask a woman at the American embassy. Like I say, nobody will see the certificate if we don't want them to."

"Oh, Mustafa, I'm so excited! When can we do this?"

"Probably tomorrow, or the next day, at the latest. But there's something else we need to talk about, before we marry."

"Yes?"

"It's about our future, sweetheart. Especially about *your* future. For one thing, when we go back to Tehran as man and wife, a lot of people are going to be unhappy. Especially your family members. They'll start gossiping behind our backs. They'll wonder why this beautiful heir to the Khamenei future and fortune would marry an *Arab* from Lebanon—"

"Excuse me, Mustafa. I don't care about those things. I care about *us*. Sure, when my grandfather dies, I'll inherit a bunch of money—unless he disowns me because I've married you. But that's very unlikely. He loves me more than anyone else, and I love him too, in an odd sort of way."

"What do you men, *odd*?"

"It's a family thing. When I was a little girl, Grandpa would hold me on his lap and sing to me, and he let me tug at his beard, no kidding! And when I reached my teens he became

103

very protective; he worried about my safety, he would ask questions about boyfriends: did I have one, what kind of person was he, that sort of thing.

"But deep down—and I've never spoken of this until now—I'm very uncomfortable about the way he and his people are leading our country. Everybody knows that Iran has a terrible reputation. It's accused of being the world's principal sponsor of worldwide terrorism. Our economy is in free fall, and we're losing money every day when we support Hezbollah here in Lebanon. As an example, when I came through immigration control at the airport the other day, the officer stared at me as though I was some kind of criminal! Just because I showed him an Iranian passport!"

"Yes, I understand that. And that leads to the next question, doesn't it?"

"What do you mean?"

"What I mean is this. Do you *really* want to spend the rest of your life living in Iran, as it is now being run by your grandfather and his advisers? You're welcome to stay here, with me, in Lebanon, but I doubt you would want that."

"No, of course I want to go home, with *you!*"

"Okay. Let's say we do that, and after we've been in Tehran for some time, you—we—decide to try to change things, slowly, for the better. Don't forget, sweetheart, you're a very popular person in your country. People will listen to what you have to say."

"I'm not sure I understand."

"Hmm. You can look at it this way. After we've been living in Tehran, say for a few months, you decide to call in some friends, people your age, and you talk to them. You tell them you're concerned about your country's future and, likely, they'll agree with you. Heck, most of your friends—probably every one of them—has an iPhone. They know what's going on in America and Europe. They know those places are spoken of as the free world. And that most certainly does *not* include Iran.

"You could organize a small group of friends, young people who think and act the way you do. Each one of them, in turn, talks to their friends, and so on. Pretty soon you would have a network reaching throughout the city, young people all talking about the same things. Believe it, sweetheart, this is the way politics works in the free world!"

"You know, Mustafa, that's another reason I love you so much. You really are a visionary, a man who wants to do good things for this world.

"But now, back to our wedding. You spoke of an American you know. What's that all about?"

"Yes, that *is* important. You should know as much about this man as I do. His name is Tony Matthews and he's an American intelligence officer. He has an office right here in Beirut, at the American embassy. I spoke with him a few days ago, and I told him about you and me—"

"You what? To an American *spy*?"

"Trust me, Roya. This man is a straight arrow. He and his people in Washington—we all want the same thing—an Iran that is free, efficient, and prosperous. And he believes—as do I—that you and I can help make that happen. Please, sweetheart, let's the two of us meet Mr. Matthews, and then you can decide. Our wedding is one thing, but our future—and Iran's future—are another and much more important."

"Okay, Mustafa. There's no harm in meeting the man if, as you say, he can help us get married. But I'm going to wait and see about the rest of it."

* * *

The next morning, in the American embassy's waiting room.

"Good morning. I'm Tony Matthews, and you are Roya Khamenei. I'm so glad you agreed to come here this morning. After learning about you from Mustafa, I wasn't sure that would happen, but I'm grateful that you're here."

"Thank you, Mr. Matthews. Yes, it was a difficult decision, but my fiancé told me you can help us with our wedding, and that's very important to both of us. As for the other subject we're likely to discuss, I'm open, even if skeptical."

"Yes, I expected you to speak frankly. From what little I know about you, that's part of your nature.

"Mustafa, how much have you said to Roya about your wedding?"

"Just speculation. I know you're familiar with the churches here in Beirut, but we don't have to be married in a church. And we're not interested in having an imam do it. A civil ceremony would be fine."

"Good. I know an American professor at AUB. He teaches religion and philosophy, and he's a licensed clergyman. I'm certain he'll be willing to do it, after he's heard from me."

"What about witnesses? We need two, don't we?"

"I believe that's so. But it's not a problem. I can be one and my administrative assistant can be the other. Roya, how does this sound to you?"

"It's beautiful. But as soon as the ceremony is over—and before our honeymoon—I want to come back here and talk about that other 'thing,' if you know what I mean."

* * *

It was a beautiful, if subdued, ceremony, held in the university's chapel, with only five people present. The two returned to her hotel and enjoyed a quiet, poolside dinner. It was Roya's first experience with champagne, and she admitted she loved it.

The next morning they returned to the American embassy, as Roya had insisted. Tony Matthews as waiting for them. Their meeting would either confirm or deny his better judgment.

* * *

"Welcome, once again. Roya, I thought your wedding ceremony was perfect. For what it's worth, I believe you chose the perfect man to marry. You and Mustafa have a great future ahead of you, and anything we can do to help make that a reality, just ask."

"Thank you, Mr. Matthews. Yes, I suppose you're right. But I've concluded that our future will depend a good deal on what we talk about, in the 'here and now,' as you Americans say.

"What you're suggesting is that, after Mustafa and I have returned to Tehran, I will become—how do you say it?—an *agent* for the Central Intelligence Agency? You must know that if I'm discovered in this role, I could be accused of treason, notwithstanding that I'm part of Iran's royal family. And I don't need to remind you what happens to Persians who commit treason. Our sharia legal system routinely demands that the accused be put to death, usually by stoning."

"Mustafa, have you discussed this with Roya?"

"At great length, actually. She and I are equally concerned about Iran's future. So much so, in fact, that we're willing to accept those risks. And in one sense, because I'm an Arab Lebanese, not a Persian, my risk may be even greater."

'Because?"

"Because if I'm found out, it amounts to one of your agency's spies being uncovered. That amounts to *international* espionage.

You can imagine how the Tehran media would play that up, and within hours the entire world would know. Our pictures would be posted on Facebook and Instagram, and anyone with a smartphone or a computer could read and see the whole sordid picture."

"Yes, you're absolutely right about that. But let me try to assure you, each of you, that we've done a thorough assessment of the risks that you've mentioned."

"Good, we're listening."

"The CIA, as you might imagine, has hundreds of assets in dozens of countries. You almost never hear about this and in those rare instances when you do, it's because a local security service—in your case that would be VAJA—has uncovered the activity. We believe the chances of that happening with VAJA are virtually zero. And here's why.

"First, at my headquarters in Washington, DC, probably no more than four people will know anything about you two. We have a system called need to know or compartmentation. That means *only* those officials who have an absolute need to know are privy to your existence.

"Second, all of the communication about you two goes by encoded messaging. No one, but no one, sees this material except, again, those four officials. And even they don't know your real names because we assign a code name to each one of you.

"Third, after you've settled down in Tehran, you'll begin to renew friendships. Your friends—especially Roya's friends—will be curious and exited to learn about your love affair, your marriage, and your plans for your future. When you're comfortable with the idea, you can begin to suggest that you sense growing dissatisfaction about the way the government is leading Iran. You can encourage your friends to speak openly about their concerns. When you learn something new or important, you can text it to us with your iPhone.

"Fourth, of course we need a means to communicate with each other. And here's how we do that. You see these two iPhones? They look like any other iPhone, but they're not the same. Our technicians have altered these iPhones just for you two. Roya, your iPhone has an icon in the upper left corner, an image of the ruins at Persepolis. You tap that icon, and it asks for a passcode, a four-digit number of your choosing.

"Mustafa, your iPhone has an icon but with a different image; this one is of the Cedars of Lebanon.

"The moment you enter that four-digit passcode, my communications center picks up the signal and begins an automatic recording. You can either text or speak; either one works. And it's the same 24/7, seven days a week."

"Can we use these phones to talk to each other?"

'Yes. To do that you enter a different passcode. And when you do that, an automatic voice scrambler activates so that no one but you two can understand what is being said.

"Now, this system works in both directions. When we have a message for you—and we expect that, eventually, there will be many of them—your iPhones will emit a distinctive ringtone. When you hear that tone, you tap in the same four-digit passcode, and the message is ready to download to your phone. I should emphasize that this is the most important part of our communications link because we'll be forwarding information to you two from a number of other sources, things that you'll need to know about."

"Who's paying for all of this? And how?"

"Good question, Mustafa. As soon as you feel comfortable with your new surroundings, you can drop a few hints that you've made profitable investments in Beirut, say in Lebanese real estate. For Roya, everyone assumes she doesn't need new money, because she's part of the royal family.

"Then you go to your central bank, the Bank Melli, and open an account. After you've done that you send us the routing and account numbers. Then, when you need new funds, you go on the internet and key in this account number. It's a legitimate bank in Beirut but one in which we have several accounts, none of them traced to the US government.

"The account, of course, is in Lebanese pounds but the bank will wire back the equivalent amount in rials."

"What kind of expenses are you thinking about?"

"Yes, I was coming to that. You probably will want to rent an apartment, or a small single-family home, not to live in—that will be up to Roya—but for your meetings with friends and other guests. At least one room in this dwelling can be used for your clinic, a place where children will be welcomed for physical checkups.

"You'll need a license, but we assume the authorities will provide one, as soon as they learn that you're Roya's husband."

"Before we leave, there's one more thing, Mr. Matthews. And it might be important."

"Certainly, Roya. What is it?"

"It's about my brother, Hussein. Unfortunately, he's an alcoholic, he can't keep a job—although he doesn't need one—and he hangs out with some people who cause me to worry. I know he has a friend in our palace guard system—he's actually a VAJA agent—and he probably has friends in the Quds Force. To be frank, my brother and I don't like each other. He thinks I'm a spoiled brat, and he's very jealous. So you might keep that in mind; perhaps your people can do something about it."

* * *

Their Iran Air flight from Beirut was uneventful, except for the loud applause that erupted throughout the cabin when one of the flight attendants announced that a "royal couple" was aboard. As soon as the Airbus 330 touched down, Roya phoned her grandfather's aide and asked him to send a car to the airport.

"Tell Grandpa I'm home, I'm safe, and I have a husband. His name is Mustafa Shadid, and Grandpa will love him!"

An hour later the newlyweds arrived at Roya's apartment. It would be their home until they found something more suitable.

Eleven

Wednesday, July 18, 2018, 0930 hours, CIA Headquarters, in the office of Sam Wolters, Chief, Near East Division.

"Tom, I presume you've read the latest message from Beirut?"

"Just did, Sam. It looks like a good news/bad news thing. The good news is really great news. We now have what amounts to a penetration of Iran's royal family."

"Yeah, we have to give a lot of credit to Tony Matthews and his new friend, this Mustafa guy. They persuaded the ayatollah's granddaughter to sign on with us, and, Lord knows, she's taking one heck of a risk to do that."

"I'm concerned about the 'bad news' part of this message."

"The brother?"

"For sure. But I think this op has enough potential that we can get the Seventh Floor to agree to task NSA."

"I'm thinking the same thing. We need to have a way to monitor the chatter that's likely to come up very soon, as soon as Roya and her husband begin to go to work."

"What do you think? We use one of our own birds, or ask NSA to task one of theirs?"

"Fortunately, the NSA people I know about couldn't care less. Even if we use our latest KH-40 satellite, NSA will do the deciphering and readout. And it's all electronic, instantaneous.

Our comm center gets the material the moment NSA does the decryption."

"What about specific targets?"

"It's a short list: The ayatollah's compound, just off Ferdowsi Square. Last I heard they use three UHF antennas. Second would be the VAJA headquarters building, and I think NSA already has a handle on that target. Third would be the Quds Force building, and, like the other two, our satellite imagery has pinpointed its location."

"Sam, there may be one other target. Kind of a long shot, but probably worth trying."

"Yeah, you're right about that. The nightclub the brother goes to. What's it called?"

"Jordan's Place. NSA's had no reason, yet, to target that location, but we can ask them to add it to their list. That would be mostly cell phone chatter, but it's probably not encoded, so they can read it directly and send us summaries."

"They do voice recognition?"

"They do, but unless real names are picked up, it won't help much."

"Okay, Tom. You know the drill. Write up a formal ops proposal, I'll take it to the DDO, and he'll probably want the DCI to sign off. And we need a bigot list. Remember, Tony Matthews promised these two that only four people will know about this. We've already stretched that number to six, but the way these things go around here, that's not bad."

Twelve

1100 hours, in the office of DDO Adam Cartwright.

"C'mon in, Sam, Sally told me you're on your way. What's up?"

"Adam, you've probably seen some of the traffic from Beirut. Now it's time we get serious about this. I've asked my deputy to write up an ops proposal, and I have it right here, in my hot little hand. You can easily imagine how concerned we are about keeping the lid on this operation. Our guys have managed to develop a penetration of Iran's royal palace, if I can put it that way, and it's imperative that no one, but no one—except you and two or three others—learn about this. It has to be okay for you to brief the director, but I'd do it so no one else is there, and above all he doesn't tell anyone, not even SecState. But because this whole thing was the president's idea—command, actually—the director can tell him we're making progress but still have a long way to go."

"I would agree with that. What else?"

"As you read this ops proposal you'll notice that we've given Beirut the okay to issue our latest modified iPhones to both the granddaughter and her husband. We've also authorized a Lebanese bank account on which they can draw funds as they need them. And we've not placed a limit on this, which is most unusual."

"What about commo security?"

"Assuming you approve, I'm going to stop by our comm center and ask to talk to Charlie Gibson. As you know, he runs that place, and he can see to it any traffic from Beirut—about this operation—gets Code One handling. That means it's not decrypted until it gets to my office, so even the comm center people don't see it. And that's about as tight as we can make it."

"Sounds good, my friend. Go for it!"

Thirteen

VAJA headquarters, 1446 Amanpoor Avenue, Tehran. Ali Younesi, veteran VAJA director, has summoned his deputy, Hadar Sohrab.

"Hadar, I've just received a message from Beirut. I want you to read it, and then we'll talk about it. Even though its author isn't identified, you'll remember that sleeper informant that we hear from now and then. He's turned up something that has enormous potential but not without some serious risks."

"Hmm, yes, I can see that. He somehow learned that our supreme leader's granddaughter is in Beirut and that she and a man walked into the American embassy. He assumes the man is either a good friend or possibly her husband, judging from the way they responded to each other. And they were inside the building for more than thirty minutes, much longer than needed to ask for directions."

"Yes. From the other details he's provided, we have to believe that those two spoke with an American official. Why would they do that?"

"They certainly wouldn't want to emigrate to America. That kind of scandal would make instant worldwide news, and they would be regarded as traitors here in Tehran. No, there's another explanation, and we should learn what it is."

"You're thinking surveillance?"

"Yes and I believe I have the authority to do that on my own initiative, without seeking approval from higher up."

"If you—we—were to be found out, then what?"

"My relationship with the ayatollah is good enough to withstand the storm. I would tell him what we just learned, and he'd understand. He wouldn't like it, but he wouldn't have much choice."

"What kind of surveillance?"

"Easy steps. We bug Roya's residence and tap her telephone. Although, like most young people in this city, she probably uses an iPhone or some other wireless device. Depending on what that tells us, we can begin to watch her movements. Who does she visit, who comes to her home, what do they talk about?"

"I'm sure you know what you're doing, but if our supreme leader learns of this and you haven't told him, it could be very bad."

"True, my friend. But think of it this way. Let's assume that Roya and her man friend were given an assignment while they were inside that embassy building. That would mean they have agreed to spy on their own country for the Americans. What's the punishment for that?"

"Stoning, in the public square."

"Okay. I'm asking you to task our technical people. Find out where she's living, and go from there."

* * *

Her name was Bahar Sohrab, Hadar's wife. Although he should have known better, Hadar often talked to his wife about his work, and this morsel was too good to keep to herself: an order to conceal a microphone in the home of Roya Khamenei, the supreme leader's granddaughter? What Hadar had overlooked: Their daughter, Esfir Sohrab, had grown up with Roya. They'd been best friends all through their school years and still were very close.

As she thought about it, Bahar decided this wasn't fair: snooping on the ayatollah's granddaughter. What possible reason could the Iranian intelligence service have for doing such an awful thing?

No, this is wrong. I'm going to tell Esfir what I've just learned, and she, I am sure, will tell Roya.

* * *

In another wing of the VAJA headquarters building.

"I have an appointment with your personnel officer. I wasn't given his name, only that I should appear at this time and in this office."

"Your name?"

"Sure, it's Abdullah Safavi, date and place of birth February 23, 1987, Isfahan."

"One moment, please, while I check …. Yes, I see you're scheduled to meet with Amir Modani, and he's expecting you. Room 4315."

"Thanks. You can tell Mr. Modani I'm on my way."

* * *

"Welcome, Mr. Safavi. I've gone over your application and have one question. Perhaps others will follow. Why are you requesting a transfer from our foreign office?"

"Thanks for seeing me, Mr. Modani. The answer is pretty simple. Even though I told my superiors I thought I was ready for an overseas assignment, that opportunity was never offered. They knew I can speak French and English, but it didn't seem to matter. I'm assuming that if I'm accepted, VAJA might have overseas opportunities."

"That's true, but first you have to go through a six-month internship. During that period you'll learn as much as we can teach you about counterintelligence, how we protect our service and our secrets from our enemies, primarily the Israelis and the Americans."

"That sounds fine, but before I do that, I have a question that's been on my mind for some time."

"And that is?"

"Does our service, VAJA, have any responsibility for investigating corruption in our country's government? This is a well-known problem, not just here but wherever people pay attention to Iran. And frankly, I'm concerned about it because it's bound to be hurting our reputation in foreign capitals."

"*Frankly*, Mr. Safavi, it's a touchy subject. It's touchy because this corruption of which you speak exists in nearly every department of government, usually among the leaders of those departments. And as you might imagine, if VAJA were to pursue this issue—really pursue it—we'd no doubt be ordered to stop. These are very powerful men, and they won't put up with the embarrassing exposure that would result."

"What about undisclosed investigations? We could collect information and withhold its release until we have enough to bring before a court."

"In theory, that would be the way to go. But truth be told, there are very few jurists in our system—especially here, in Tehran—who would be willing to do that. They could lose their positions were they to accept such cases."

"What if I were to do some digging on my own while I'm in this internship program? No one needs to know about it, except you, of course. I could do it on my own time and report directly to you, say, once a month. Then, after some time, you can decide if it's worth pursuing."

"Yes, I can agree to that, Mr. Safavi, but if you're discovered I won't be able to help. And you would almost certainly be asked to resign your position."

"That's okay. It's a risk I'm willing to take."

* * *

That evening, before going to bed, Abdullah Safavi retrieved his iPhone and made a call. His friends in Ankara and Washington, DC, would be well pleased.

* * *

"Look at this, Tom, our VAJA penetration has called in for the first time!"

"Pretty amazing, the man's ingenuity, to get himself a special, low-risk assignment when he hasn't yet put in a full day at the office."

"It's low-risk until he gets caught. But apparently he doesn't expect that to happen."

"We've got our work cut out for us. He wants us to recommend those officials he should interview. I can do a quick check with RID, see what they have."

"Good idea. I'd start with ministry chiefs, or better still, Khameini's inner circle, his so-called cabinet—*if* they're willing to talk to him."

"You know, Sam, I should think they would be willing. Our man may be new to this job, but he's no kid. He's in his mid-thirties and has been around the block a few times. The people he interviews won't know that, only that he's speaking for VAJA, and most officials would be reluctant to refuse to talk to a representative of their own intelligence service."

"You're right about that. Okay, let's see what RID has. —What, its database is up to five hundred terabytes by now!"

* * *

The following morning.

"Okay, Sam, here's the first run. Two names, each one a ministry head:

1. Behrouz Akhtar. Minister of Finance and Banking;

2. Fareed Gilani. Minister of Agriculture."

"No Quds Force names on that list?"

"No, they're part of the Revolutionary Guards group, and I assumed those guys would never cooperate with our source."

"Okay, let's send him the list and see what happens."

Fourteen

Tuesday, July 31, 2018, 0930 hours, in the office of Sam Wolters, Chief, Near East Division.

"Tom, I've just come from a meeting with our boss. The DDO believes—and he's right—that we're moving too slowly on this regime change operation. He wants us to find at least one additional asset to add to our agent pool, preferably a young male Muslim who can quickly assimilate with the local Persian population. And not necessarily in Tehran. As we talked about it, we agreed that it wouldn't hurt to focus on Mashhad. As you know, that's Iran's second city, regarded as one of its holiest with that Goharshad mosque and the Imam Ali mausoleum.

"So we need to find a young Shia Muslim, preferably a guy without a track record, someone who won't come up on VAJA's radar should he ever come to their attention."

"If our target city is going to be Mashhad, why not stay close to home? Our station in Ashkhabad would be the place to start looking. Who's in charge out there? We rarely hear from them."

"It's a small station, only three guys. The COS is Tom Russell. I know Tom, slightly. He's a good officer, speaks Farsi *and* Arabic, and he's been on post for about two years, so he should have an idea or two about how to do this."

* * *

1700 hours, Sunday, January 2, 2017, Mashhad, Iran. Dr. Farhad Rafati has excused his last patient and is preparing to go home for the day.

"Bahar, I'm leaving early today, but I'll be here tomorrow, about nine. Do you have my first patient scheduled?"

"Yes, I do. Her name is Roshan Kirmani. She's thirty-six years old and is complaining of severe headaches; she's had them for two months. They won't go away, and she believes it could be some kind of psychological disorder. And she knows that's one of your specialties."

"Okay, Bahar, if she gets here before I do, please have her wait. The forecast calls for snow tonight and early tomorrow morning, so it's possible I'll be a little bit late."

* * *

Bahar Kirmani had been the doctor's do-it-all assistant for five years, going on six. She admired the man, being careful not to admire him *too* much. He was handsome and still single, and her Muslim faith would frown on any kind of office romance. Still, she wondered about the man. She knew, as did a few of his patients, that he was fabulously rich, and he certainly didn't need to work for a living. Shortly after she came to work for him, he had confided that his grandfather had invested heavily in the Anglo-Iranian Oil Company, and by the time it was nationalized by Muhammad Mosaddeq in 1953, his share holdings were worth something close to 7.5 million rials. Eventually, the doctor inherited this wealth. He had had the good sense to convert it to gold bullion, where it was being held in Paris in a vault at the Bred Banque Populaire. As long as the mullahs in Tehran continued to allow currencies to flow without restriction, he was home free.

Bahar had another reason to admire her employer. His clinic was open for business three days a week: Saturday, Sunday, and Monday. He devoted Tuesday, Wednesday and Thursday to a shelter for as many of Mashhad's indigents as could squeeze in, sometimes as many as fifty, usually thirty or forty. It wasn't long before Farhad Rafati had established a reputation as the city's leading philanthropist. Even the city's mullahs had to admit that his ability to heal broken spirits far outpaced their sermons about the healing powers of Allah's mercies.

But then the Mashhad city council decided that Farhad Rafati had become *too* successful, and they imposed a one-of-a-kind tax on his business: five hundred rials a day for each patient that came to his clinic. After a few months of this the doctor realized it was too much, and he decided to move his clinic to nearby Ashkhabad, capital of Turkmenistan. He knew that much of that city's population spoke Farsi, and for those who did not, the doctor's knowledge of Arabic would be good enough. Plus, he had a cousin who lived there, a real estate salesman and a fellow Shia believer who could help him navigate his way through a likely hostile Sunni environment.

It was a huge bother, but Dr. Rafati had to fly to Tehran, there to locate the Turkmenistan consular office and apply for an entry visa. The interviewing official asked the routine questions and was surprised to learn that his visitor was one of the wealthiest men in the country and that he was about to take his wealth with him and open a clinic in Ashkhabad.

"Not a problem, doctor. I'm sure my country will welcome you with open arms."

* * *

And welcome him it did. His first order of business was to contact his bank in Paris and ask for an electronic transfer of 100,000 manats (the equivalent of 125,000 US dollars). Second, he phoned his cousin to inquire about rental properties and learned that real estate in Ashkhabad was much cheaper than he had expected. His cousin told him he had recently acquired a new listing: an unoccupied, street-level suite of offices on Kemine Street. Would that do?

Forty-eight hours later, Farhad Rafati had placed an online announcement of his new practice, set up his own web page (www.rafaticounseling.tn) and was ready to receive his first patient at 4525 Kemine Street.

* * *

Monday, 0900 hours, April 5, 2010, in the office of Thomas Russell, Chief of Station, Ashkhabad. Russell is speaking to his deputy, Nicholas Jackson.

"So Nick, what did the man have to say? You said he phoned after dinner last night and asked to see you ASAP? What happened?"

"Maybe the best lead we've had in years, Tom. He told me his cousin has just arrived in our fair city and has already opened his practice. Believe it or not, he's within walking distance of where you and I are standing, no kidding!"

"Hmm, we knew this might happen. What, after your last meeting he told you his cousin was thinking about coming to Ashkhabad?"

"True, but now that he's actually here, we need to think about recruiting the good doctor. He'd be a perfect answer to that cable we got from headquarters last month."

"And you've already asked headquarters for traces, based on what the cousin told you?"

"Yep. As you might imagine, he's a clean slate. Nobody has heard of the man, not until now."

"Our guys in Mashhad, what do they say?"

"They know he was well liked in the city. He had a part-time counseling service, and the other three days of the week he operated a homeless shelter for the city's indigents."

"And he speaks Farsi and Arabic, no English?"

"Correct. But that shouldn't be a problem. I plan to ask his cousin to broker our first meeting, next Wednesday in our safe house on Konyev Street. So the three of us can converse in Arabic."

"You plan to wear a wire?"

"I think so. That way I won't miss anything, and we'll have it as backup in case headquarters wants to listen in."

"Okay. Sounds good, let's do it!"

* * *

Thursday Morning.

"How'd it go, Nick?"

"He's a very persuasive guy, that's for sure. If he had lived anywhere but in Iran, he could have run for mayor or maybe even a governor. He has a huge beef against the authorities down there in his hometown but especially in Tehran. He thinks they're a bunch of hypocrites, dishonest, looking out only for each other and making themselves very rich in the process."

"How does he feel about going back?"

"Yeah, that idea surprised him but after I explained our reasoning he thought it made sense. I don't know the words for regime change in Arabic, but he caught on very quickly, and he likes it."

"What about methods?"

"He was ahead of me on that one. Said he could resume his practice as a counselor, but this time he'll be more aggressive about finding clients who count: government officials, a couple of imams he knows, and especially the well-heeled merchants who pretty much dominate the city's economy."

"What about Islam? Is that important to him?"

"Yes and no. He's not really a believer, and he knows enough about Christianity that he has some serious questions about Muhammad's legitimacy. And he plans to use this Sunni-Shia fight as his reason for returning to Mashhad. He'll claim he found it too difficult to try to work in a Sunni-dominated culture, and so he chose to return to his hometown where that won't be an issue."

"What about commo?"

"Not a problem. I gave him our modified iPhone, showed him how to use it. He's smart, he said it's a lot like his own iPhone. He knows that when he does use it, he'll be talking either to us or to our station in Beirut."

"Okay, write it up for headquarters. I think we're good to go."

Fifteen

Bahar Sohrab had just returned from shopping at Arzumian's meat market. Sarkis Arzumian was an Armenian merchant whose shop sold frozen pork chops imported from Yerevan. It was the only place in all of Tehran where one could buy pork of any kind. His customers assumed he was paying some kind of hush money to the local police, else his business would have been shut down years ago.

Like many modern Persian women, Bahar resented the fact that her Muslim faith prohibited the consumption of pork of any kind. One could also buy bacon at the shop and then enjoy the American favorite, bacon and eggs.

As she was putting her purchase into the kitchen's freezer, she felt the buzz of her smartphone in her pocket. That would be her daughter, Esfir, calling to catch up on the latest family news.

"Hi, sweetheart. How are you this morning? … Good. Have you settled that issue with your landlord? … Oh, he's not going to do anything about it. You reminded him that your father wouldn't like it? … Well, of course he's afraid of VAJA, everybody is. And that reminds me, Esfir, we need to talk, not on the phone but here. Why don't you come over for lunch, say about noon? … Good, I'll see you then."

* * *

"He what?"

"That's right, Esfir. He should never have talked about this, but sometimes he gets careless."

"Well, just because he saw Roya walk into an American embassy—so what?"

"Remember, sweetheart, your father is a very powerful man in this country. He can't afford to be wrong, especially where the royal family is involved. He made his decision because he wants to be certain."

"So why are you telling me this?"

"Because I believe Roya should know about it. You are her best friend, after all, and she'll believe you and respect you for sharing our secret."

"Did Father do this without telling anyone? If Roya's family should learn of it, he might lose his job!"

"He said he's confident he'll be believed and the ayatollah would understand."

"If I tell Roya, as you suggest, will Father know?"

"Absolutely not. This is strictly between you and me."

"Okay. I'll call her, and we'll meet at my place. That should be safe enough."

* * *

Three days later, in Roya's apartment.

"Hey, Roya, what's this with the water running full blast into the kitchen sink?"

"Shh. We need to go outside. Something awful has happened."

The newlyweds stepped outside and onto Roya's patio. They sat on a bench with their backs to the sliding glass doors.

"What's going on, Roya? You're frightened, that's for sure."

"I had lunch with Esfir, at her place. She said her father—he's the head man at VAJA, remember—has ordered that they put hidden microphones in our home. Whether they've done this already, I don't know."

"Wait a minute. Why would they do that?"

"Because somebody saw us go into the American embassy, when we were in Beirut. Whoever it was said we were inside the building long enough that they've concluded we're somehow helping the Americans. *Spying*, in other words."

"Okay, let's assume they *have* already done it. We can be careful about what we talk about, and we can step outside now and then. But I'm going to use our iPhone and report this. We need some advice about what to do next."

* * *

One hour later in the office of Sam Wolters.

"Tom, get to your monitor, quick, and have a look."

"Yeah, maybe the wheels are coming off the wagon. What do you think?"

"Well, we know the comm link works; Beirut has the same message, as does Ashkhabad."

"This is our first contact with these folks, and they want our advice."

"I can think of several possibilities; maybe you can, too."

"One would be to advise Roya to go to her grandfather and raise hell about this. I'd bet a week's salary that the VAJA people haven't told the royals what they're up to."

"Or we could ask her and her new husband to pretend they know nothing about the bugs and feed some misleading info to VAJA."

"Such as?"

"She could hint that she knows the VAJA chief—what's his name, Ali Younesi—is shacking up with Khameini's secretary. We have pictures of her, and she's a real beauty, considering her age."

"Not a bad idea. That would tie them in knots for a month, maybe more."

"And even if their investigation goes nowhere, they can't get back to Roya. If they do that, then they'll have to admit they have her home bugged. I think it's a win-win deal."

"Okay, let's do it."

* * *

The next morning, on Roya's outdoor patio.

"Roya, look at this. We have an answer already!"

"Yes, Mustafa. I see the same message on my phone."

"What do you think? Is this something you'd be comfortable with?"

"I like the idea but not the people they suggest. I know Banu Safavi, she's my grandfather's secretary, a very sweet and loyal woman. No, she won't do."

"Anyone else?"

"Yes, as a matter of fact. There's a woman—what's her name?— Azar Khavan—she's married to Jamshid Rostami, the head of our foreign office, our country's top diplomat. I've never liked either one of those two; they're so snobbish and self-centered, always trying to give the impression that they're in charge of

Iran's foreign policy. My grandfather feels the same way, but he decided some time ago that to dismiss him would create too much friction with the other cabinet members."

"Okay. So this evening, while we're having dinner, you can talk about this. You tell me what you just said, how you don't like Mr. Rostami, that you know he's sleeping with one of the younger women who work in the foreign office. You don't need to name her, but when VAJA listens to our conversation, they'll have to open an investigation. They'll call in Rostami and interrogate him. He'll deny everything, but the process will waste months of time and effort."

"I like that, Mustafa. Why don't you respond, first thing in the morning, with the changes we've talked about."

* * *

Two days later in the office of Sam Wolters.

"Tom, I'm beginning to realize what a gold mine we have in these two. They're thinking like you or I would, if our roles were reversed."

"I agree with that. Maybe it's time we triggered our arrangement with our friends at NSA. They have a fix on the VAJA headquarters building in Tehran. Can you do that on your own, or does the DDO have to sign off?"

"No. When we first discussed this possibility, he told me I'm free to do it on my own. I'll have to go down the hall to the vault; there's a secure line in there that goes directly to Fort Meade."

"How do they process the take?"

"It all records to disc, automatically. Then one of their translators will turn it into English and give us a tape."

Seventy-two hours later.

"Here's the first batch, Tom. Strap on those earphones, and have a listen. There are two voices, one apparently VAJA's top guy, Ali Younesi, and he's speaking to a subordinate. You'll love this."

"What the hell is going on here?! Our highly esteemed Foreign Minister is shacking up with one of his staff people?"

"Sounds like he's really enjoying himself. The woman is in her thirties apparently, and he's what? Sixty-five?"

"Yeah, and he's paying her. Fifty thousand rials for thirty minutes!"

"Let's hope she thinks she's worth more than that."

"So what do we do with this? We can't admit that we have this bug working."

"No, we haul his ass in here and accuse him of screwing this young woman. We don't need her name, just the accusation will be enough."

"Yeah, he'll come to the conclusion that VAJA is all-seeing and all-knowing, and that's exactly what we want him to think."

"We could demand that he resign, couldn't we?"

"That's a decision I can't make. We'd have to get the ayatollah's permission, and to do that I'd have to admit that we have a bug in his granddaughter's home. So no, we just sit on this and let the poor bastard sweat."

* * *

"What now, Sam?"

"First, we thank our NSA friends and ask them to keep up the good work. Then, we send a message to our two miracle workers in Tehran and tell them they're doing exactly what we've been hoping for. They don't need to know about the Fort Meade intercept operation, only that the fun and games in their bugged apartment are working perfectly."

Sixteen

0800 hours, Monday, February 5, 2017, Mashhad, Iran. Dr. Farhad Rafati is speaking to an old friend in his real estate office on Avenue Ferdowsi.

"So Farhad, I see you've decided to return to your old stomping grounds. How come?"

"Tell you what, Bijan, if you've ever tried to live in a place where you're surrounded by Sunni Muslims, you'd understand. It was a real pain."

"I can imagine. I've heard stories about that sort of thing. But what can I do for you? I assume you need a place to live."

'Yeah, I'm sorry now that I sold my clinic. But I'd like to find something similar. Do you have any listings that would fit?"

"Let me check my computer, shouldn't take very long. —Ah, yes, there *is* a place that's for rent or sale, whichever you prefer. Pretty much like the one you sold; same number of rooms, ground level, and it's partially furnished. The pair who worked there were real estate consultants, people I know slightly, in fact."

"Good. I'll take your word for it. Do I pay you or deal with the owners?"

"I can handle it. I'll take my usual 7 percent; the rest goes to them. I don't want to be prying, but what do you intend to do, now that you've returned?"

"Good question and I can answer it truthfully because we're good friends. I think you know from our previous conversations how I feel about those idiots in Tehran. I don't have a quarrel with Khamenei; he's doing his best to hold our country together. It's all the people beneath him who are at fault. You've heard the stories; ministers on the take from the groups they're supposed to regulate, hyperinflated prices in the Grand Bazaar with each senior merchant taking at least 25 percent off the top, fudged construction contracts that result in poorly constructed—and dangerous—office buildings. It makes you think they're operating with the Italian mafia's playbook.

"Anyway, I intend to attract people to my clinic who matter. I'll start with Mashhad's mayor. I've known him for ten years, and we trust each other. There are more than twenty-five counties in Khorasan Province, each headed by a local politician. And I'm guessing our mayor knows every one of them. Khorasan is the largest political division in all of Iran, not by population—that honor belongs to Tehran—but it's very typical, a good cross-section representation of the country."

* * *

Sixty day later, Farhad Rafati is seated at his computer's keyboard and prepares this report. Upon completion he uploads it to his iPhone and sends it to CIA headquarters.

"Quchan: Spoke with mayor who admits to overseeing a sewer construction contact that failed to meet minimum specifications. One hundred homes are now without adequate sewage facilities.

"Bojnurd: City council has refused to install traffic lights at major intersections, insisting that stop signs are adequate. In the past sixty days there have been six traffic fatalities at these same intersections.

"Shirvan: City's water supply has tested positive for presence of fecal matter; local hospital reports ten patients admitted for amoebic dysentery, three in critical condition. Mayor has refused to accept responsibility, claiming repair contractor is at fault. Four of the ten patients are about to sue the hospital.

"Sabsevar: City's high school building damaged by fire; five students and three faculty suffered third-degree burns. City fire department's investigation revealed that insurance policy had lapsed, leaving city's treasury in debt (approx fifty million rials). Insurance company auditor believes Sabsevar city manager deliberately defaulted on policy.

"Razavi: City's prison is overcrowded; some inmates have refused to eat until conditions improve. City's mayor is convinced that warden has been pocketing funds that would otherwise relieve the situation."

* * *

John Sager

In the office of Sam Wolters.

"Tom, here's the latest report from Mashhad. The good doctor is doing just what we expected of him, and he's doing it very well. It's a small sample, for sure, but it all points in the same direction: widespread corruption in just about every facet of life, at least in his Khorasan Province. I'm going to forward this, as is, to our team in Tehran. She can use it as more evidence when she's ready for her chat with her grandfather.

Seventeen

They were exhausted but satisfied. The taxi ride from the airport to their hotel was the easiest part. After their week of briefings and orientation in a northern Virginia safe house, the agency's travel office had arranged the whole thing, two Canadian citizens flying to Tehran to join the local Red Crescent office on a kind of "mercy mission," already approved by Iran's foreign minister. After two nights in the Persepolis Hotel on Kazvin Avenue, they'd be on their own.

* * *

"Hey, sweetheart, that was really cool, the way you used your Farsi to get through immigration and customs control."

"They say 'practice makes perfect,' don't they?"

"True. And I think it's safe enough to talk here. The Iranians have no reason to suspect us as being other than what we claim to be, and to bug every room in this hotel would be unlikely."

"What about a rental car? We'll need one."

"I asked the hotel concierge about that when we checked in. He said he'd have it arranged first thing in the morning."

"And the Red Crescent people know we're here?"

"I believe they do, but if they don't, I have their phone number. I know they're expecting us, but they may not have an arrival date."

"And the Beirut station has arranged for more medical supplies to arrive, about now? And the brochure?"

"That's what I understand. The brochure is designed to let people know that the Red Crescent office is expanding its services, and it encourages parents to bring in their children for routine checkups. Its subtly designed to appeal to people with low or no income, so the authorities know we're not competing with established hospital or clinic services."

"So to review the bidding, when a parent brings in his or her child, I take the kid to an examining room while you talk to the parent. You ask questions about the family's life history, it's living quarters, employment status, how it feels about available medical care and other government services. You'll have about fifteen minutes to cover the bases, and your purpose is to learn whether the family is satisfied with life in Tehran. If not, you suggest that things are likely to get better, but it will take time and patience."

"Exactly so, just like the agency's psych war officer explained it to us."

"And at the end of each day you'll add an entry to your log book, summarizing what happened. Eventually, those records will be transmitted to CIA headquarters. What they do with them, we don't need to know."

* * *

Abdul Nazari's log book begins here.

Saturday morning, January 13, 2018.

We awakened to a fresh snowfall, twenty centimeters covering the sidewalk. The mountains to the north are glistening white. Still, I wanted the clinic to remain open, believing that the Abbasi family would show up. Alborz Abbasi had come to the clinic last week, bringing his six-year-old son, Mustafa. At the time the youngster had a terrible cold, and I thought I detected an oncoming pneumonia. Alborz lost his job six months ago, in a dispute with his employer, something about poor working conditions, so the family is without a paycheck. Still, they know the clinic doesn't charge for visits. It's something paid for by the Red Crescent's many donors, most of them in Canada and the United States.

Well, he did show, about 10:00 o'clock, and I immediately sent him to Suzanne, in the next room. She's very good at this sort of thing, and after thirty minutes she decided it wasn't going to be pneumonia after all. She gave Mustafa some over-the-counter cold medicine and handed him her iPhone after finding a video game, and for the next fifteen minutes he was in digital heaven.

While that's going on, I'm talking to Alborz, Mustafa's dad. He's really down in the dumps about his job, says he hates the system here in Tehran and would give anything to move— anywhere but here. He and his wife haven't been to a mosque service in four months; he said the preaching there gives neither of them any hope.

When I asked him what might be done about this, he smiled and said he'd like most of all to see some new faces in the royal palace. The current ayatollah is too old to be in charge of a nation of more than eighty million people.

How does he feel about his own neighborhood? Is it safe there?

He knows by name the three police officers who come by, at least three times a day. They're a friendly bunch, but they complain, sometimes bitterly, about the low pay and difficult working conditions, walking their beats sometimes ten hours a day with only a thirty-minute lunch break.

I notice he carries a cell phone, and I ask him what he does with it. He mostly listens to Western music; sometimes he'll hear a Voice of America broadcast, and when it's in Farsi he's really happy about that. The VOA people tell their Iranian listeners that it's only a matter of time until the mullahs and the ayatollah will turn over everything to a more reasonable form of government.

That's the kind of opening I always look for because now I can tell him that we Canadians are hoping, and praying, for the same thing.

About now, Suzanne is through with her examination of young Muhammad and the two of them leave the clinic. The sun has broken through, and the snow is beginning to melt. They'll likely be back next week, just to chat if nothing else.

* * *

Monday morning, January 15, 2018.

Kind of a different situation, today. About 11:00 this morning I heard the doorbell and opened the door, and there stood Amaya Hashemi and her ten-year-old daughter Shahnaz. At first I didn't recognize either of them because it had been six months since they were last here. But Amaya remembered, and as she was very worried about her daughter, she persuaded a neighbor to drive all the way from South Tehran. That's where they live, in one of the city's poorest neighborhoods.

She explained that since their last visit her daughter has become sort of a tomboy, preferring to play with boys rather than girls. One of her boy-buddies showed her how to shoot marbles, and soon a small group of them were having friendly competitions. Down on their knees in the nearest vacant lot, Shahnaz shot a marble and missed its target, the marble coming to a stop in a slight depression in the dirt. She reached for the marble, and much to her surprise she realized that she was disturbing a half-asleep scorpion. In self-defense, it stung her right thumb, now swollen to twice its normal size and very, very painful.

As I recall, scorpions prefer a dry, desert-like environment, and Tehran is like that for about ten months of the year. The scorpion instinctively knows that it needs to prepare for the colder months, and to do that it digs a small depression where it hopes to avoid the cold. It was pure dumb luck that Shahnaz now is hurting like never before.

I quickly tell Suzanne what's happened, and Shahnaz disappears into Suzy's small treatment center. She later told me that she has a kind of all-purpose antidote for insect bites. Whether this will help little Shahnaz remains to be seen, but they'll know within fifteen minutes or so. While they're waiting, two Tylenol tablets should help.

I use that time to try to comfort Amaya, telling her that her daughter will be okay; it will just take some time. And I suggest, as gently as I know how, that she tell me about current living conditions in her neighborhood.

After wiping away some tears, she begins her story, and it's not a pleasant one. First, her husband left her three months ago— taking advantage of the Muslim rule as prescribed by Prophet Muhammad. "I divorce thee, please don't come back." So now she's supposed be getting a check from the government because she can prove that she's in poverty status. But she hasn't yet seen a check, and she's about out of money. Her neighbors are trying to help, but they don't have much money either.

She begins to cry again and tells me she'd give anything to move, anywhere but Tehran. She has a cousin in Isfahan, but she can't afford the trip. She says she heard a radio broadcast a few months ago in which the speaker—a man connected to the city's welfare department—promised that *any woman* who is abandoned by her husband has the right to appeal for financial help. So that's what she did. She filled out the forms and mailed them to the appropriate address, and she's still waiting.

I try to be gentle about it, but I want to know if her Muslim faith is helping during this time of maximum stress. She looks at me with that "are you kidding me?" expression, and I decide to drop it.

Then I tell her that I'm pretty sure that things are going to be much better in her country. Other people are sharing her concerns, and sooner or later, something dramatic is likely to happen.

By now, little Shahnaz is feeling much better, and the two of them leave. They'll try to catch a bus back to their neighborhood. So far, buses are the cheapest form of public transportation. Will I see them again? Only God knows.

* * *

Thursday afternoon, March 22, 2018

When Suzy and I agreed to this gig, we were warned that in a country like Iran we could expect just about anything. I'm convinced that that *anything* happened yesterday evening. Here's the story.

Yesterday, March 21, was the annual *nowruz* holiday, the Iranian nation's New Year celebration. It's not unusual for these folks to forget their Muslim faith's forbidding the use of alcohol, and many of them are dead drunk before midnight. That apparently is what happened, according to Baraz Rajavi, who showed up at our clinic's front door at nine this morning with his teenage daughter, Banu.

I could see that something was wrong with his daughter, and I asked her to step into Suzy's examining room. While she was with Suzy, Baraz told me what had happened.

Banu is fifteen, a rather pretty teenager, and several of her girlfriends had been celebrating the new year at the home of one of the parents. No booze, just tea, party hats, and loud music. A few minutes after midnight, Banu and one of her friends decided to walk home. The weather was fine, not too cold with a clear sky and a full moon. Their conversation quickly turned to the boys they had been dating—with parents' permission, of course.

They stopped at a crosswalk, and this aging Renault convertible comes screeching to a halt, right in front of them. Two guys jump out and grab Banu, force her into the car, and speed away to a nearby park. It's as dark as the inside of a coal mine in that park, there are no witnesses, and Banu suddenly finds herself being gang-raped by these two teenage punks. After a few minutes they decide they've had their jollies. They get back into the convertible and disappear.

Banu, of course, is terrified, bleeding, and hurting. She somehow finds her way home, goes into her bedroom, and cries herself to sleep. But she awakens about 3:00 a.m. and decides to tell her father about the rape.

Now, as one might imagine, Baraz is mad as hell, wants revenge and has to wait until 7:00 a.m. to call the cops. One of them shows up a few minutes later, and after hearing the story, he says there's nothing the cops can do because they don't have the names of the assailants or a reasonable description of either one. But they do advise Baraz to take his daughter to our clinic.

And that's why she and her dad came here. Suzy gave Banu the standard pregnancy test, she's okay with that but till terribly sore and frightened. Suzy, as usual, was very patient and careful, giving me time to talk to Baraz.

Turns out that Baraz Rajavi works at a local meat market. Says he's a butcher and a very good one. His wife, Ashraf, works in a beauty parlor, within walking distance of their modest home. Banu is their only child, and they have high hopes for her. She's going to be a beautiful woman in not too many years, maybe good enough to get a job in one of Tehran's modeling agencies. That's why the rape must never become known, and I promise him the secret stays within these four walls.

Then Baraz tells me about his confrontation with the local police adjutant. He's already filed an official complaint about the rape, and the adjutant looks at him as though he just fell off the turnip wagon. Obviously the adjutant won't do anything unless he gets paid and paid plenty.

He goes on to tell me that the meat inspectors are the same way. They won't certify that his product is fit for human consumption unless he pays them five thousand rials for every carcass he butchers.

I ask him what he believes to be the answer. He responds that he's persuaded the entire Iranian system is being run by a bunch of thieves, men who say they're religious and devoted to Prophet Muhammad but who, in reality, don't believe a word of it. It's all show, and unless you play this game, you'll never be able to get ahead.

I respond that I'm just one man, and a Canadian at that, but I'm convinced that this kind of dishonesty cannot prevail. Human nature, sooner or later, won't allow it.

Now it's time for Baraz and his daughter to go home. She'll be fine, bed rest for a few days, then back to normal. And Suzy and I have made two more friends, honest, hardworking people who won't forget.

Tuesday afternoon, April 17, 2018

We thought we'd seen about everything until Arman Jazani walked into the clinic yesterday morning.

He brought his six-year-old daughter Nasrin with him; she'd been complaining of headaches and a sore throat, so I immediately asked her to step into Suzanne's treatment room. As soon as we were alone, he told me that word was getting around his neighborhood about our clinic, a place to go—"for free," he said—where the treatment is good, especially for kids, and it's a place where you can let your hair down and have a good, honest chat with a Canadian guy who seems to have learned a lot about Iran. I told him I was happy to hear that, that we don't get much feedback about our services. Did *he* have anything on his mind that we could talk about while his daughter was being cared for? Yes, he certainly did.

Arman is a cobbler, has his own shop in the Abuzar Square district, about five kilometers from our clinic. He knows that his trade is almost a lost art, custom designing and making shoes and boots for wealthy clients. But the pay is good, and he's hoping he can afford to send Nasrin to a private school for girls, one of a kind in Tehran.

But it didn't take long for Arman to get around to the *real* reason for this visit, other than to help Nasrin recover from her sore throat.

Arman's wife, Yasmin, is Jewish. She was only three when she came to Iran with her parents, directly from Jerusalem. Now she's in her early forties, and the family has received word that one of her relatives is ill and not expected to live more than another month. When Yasmin visited the passport office in downtown Tehran, she was asked for her ID card, and she had nothing to show but her birth certificate. The clerk saw that she was born in Jerusalem. No, no, she wanted Yasmin's *Iranian* ID card.

So now a very flustered Yasmin had to admit that she'd never taken time to renounce her Israeli citizenship in order to apply for citizenship as an Iranian. And to make matters worse, Iran's mullahs for years had been threatening to destroy the state of Israel. The clerk looked at Yasmin as if to ask, *Do you really want to do this?*

"Yes, I do, really."

"Okay, but we have to collect a special tax because Iran and Israel don't have reciprocal agreements."

"What kind of tax?"

"Well, it's not cheap, say the equivalent of five hundred American dollars."

Yasmin does the quick mental calculation, about sixty-four *million* rials. There's no way she can possibly raise that kind of money. But wait. How about a lien on her husband's business?

As soon as she returns from Israel, the lien is removed, and everybody's happy.

Arman concludes his story with a long sigh and asks me what I think. I tell him he doesn't seem to have much wiggle room. If he can get it in writing, from an official in the passport office, Yasmin should be free to travel.

He agrees that it's worth trying and I ask him if there's anything else he'd like to talk about. Yes, he says, there is.

Arman's cobbler's shop is located on a busy street with nothing more than one of those ubiquitous sliding, corrugated steel doors to secure it when he's not there. There are three cops who patrol this street; he knows each one of them by name. Two weeks ago, one of the three told him that from now on, they each would require a thousand-rial "insurance" payment each week. Otherwise, no telling what might happen. There are lots of thieves who prowl this street in the pitch dark early-morning hours.

So now, Arman is paying these three guys, three cops who, at one time, he regarded as his friends.

I ask him, what does it mean?

Arman hangs his head, as if he's been hit by a cop's nightstick.

"You know, friend, and I hate to say this, but I'm convinced that my country has become—how to say it?—a den of thieves. And there's no end in sight, not until we get rid of these mullahs and the ayatollah. They're the ones who have to go."

I tell him that day probably is not far off. And he's likely to live to see it.

* * *

Abdul and Suzanne Nazari, after eighteen months at their Tehran clinic, have treated and interviewed nearly two hundred families. Each interview was reported to CIA headquarters where it was determined that 80 percent of them were highly critical of the regime. Summaries of these interviews were forwarded to Roya, and they became the principal motivation for her eventual confrontation with her grandfather.

Owing to the importance of the couple's contributions, they were awarded the CIA's Distinguished Service Medal in a private ceremony held in Director Franklin's office.

The couple has returned to their home in Bellevue, Washington, where Suzanne has resumed her work at Seattle's Children's Hospital. Abdul is working as a surgical nurse in Overlake Hospital.

Eighteen

As he thought about it, Abdullah Safavi realized he might be in over his head, presuming to be able to interview some of Iran's most influential officials about, of all things, corruption in their own organizations. Still, he had the backing of his VAJA superior. So he might as well get started. He decided to seek his first appointment with Behrouz Akhtar, Iran's Minister of Finance and Banking.

He made the call from his office desk and asked the operator to announce the call as coming from VAJA. That should get Mr. Akhtar's attention, and he'd be reluctant to refuse the call.

"Behrouz Akhtar here. What can I do for you?"

"Mr. Akhtar, my name is Abdullah Safavi, and I'd like to come to your office to talk about something that concerns my employer. We can't do this on the telephone, but if you're willing to give me a few minutes of your time, you'll understand my motive."

"Hmm. I've never been interviewed by someone like you, but if you say it's important then, yes, I'll be free tomorrow morning at ten o'clock."

* * *

"Thanks for accepting my request, Mr. Akhtar. This shouldn't take long, and I'll get right to the point."

"Yes, please do."

"As you know, sir, our currency is virtually worthless in the international marketplace. My service believes part of the problem can be traced to a lack of confidence on the part of overseas buyers and sellers. They believe, with some justification, that the finance and banking services in Iran are being manipulated by individuals who are lining their own pockets at the expense of their customers. This creates a lack of confidence, and that's one of the reasons—perhaps *the* reason—for the rial's downfall. What's your reaction? Are we on the right track?"

"Unfortunately, Mr. Safavi, you *are* on the right track. I'm well aware of these infractions but there's not much I can do about them."

"Why is that?"

"Probably the biggest problem is that our system now is completely digital. Every bank in the country relies on its computers to record and save to disc every transaction. If you know anything about the digital world, you can see there are unlimited opportunities for fraud and mismanagement. A bank employee, even though he might be a high school dropout, can quickly learn how to scam the system."

"In other words, sir, it's the integrity—or lack thereof—of the individual employee that's your principal problem?"

"Absolutely. And I believe there's a reason for this. You probably know that bank employees are not paid very well. Even a bank manager has less take-home pay than, say, the man across the street who runs a welding shop. And these employees talk to each other. Many of them probably resent that they can't find better jobs. And, of course, the sanctions now in place—put there by the Americans and their stooge allies—make it even more difficult."

"How about your staff, here in your ministry's headquarters?"

"I personally have chosen each one of them. A few have been with me for as long as ten years. They are honest, hardworking people, and they appreciate the fact that I have insisted on hiring women and promoting them the same way as I do men."

"Okay, Mr. Akhtar. I think that does it. You've been direct and persuasive. I'm sure my superiors will feel the same way, once they've read my report."

* * *

Back in his office, Abdullah Safavi was inclined to give himself a B-plus for his first interview. The man had been forthcoming and apparently believed he had nothing to hide. Now for the write-up. He pulled out his computer keyboard and went to work. One copy for VAJA; the other he downloaded into his iPhone, tapped the *send* icon, and waited. Ten seconds later he knew that CIA headquarters had a copy.

* * *

"Sam, this just came in from our man in Tehran. Looks like he's doing it just the way we hoped he would."

"Amen to that, Tom."

"Now that we know he's producing, have you decided what we do with his info?"

"It'll go into his case file but more to the point, we want to get this to Roya and Mustafa. One of these days she'll be visiting her grandfather, and this report, and others like it, will help her make her case."

* * *

Next case, and Abdullah Safavi hoped it would as easy as the first one. He had to admit to himself that he knew very little about Iran's agriculture or the many farmers who made it work. He consulted Iran's pirated *Google* app and did some research. That would help. Next, he asked his secretary to place a call to the office of Dr. Fareed Gilani, the Minister of Agriculture. Yes, the minister would see him at nine o'clock the next morning.

* * *

"Thank you for agreeing to this meeting, Mr. Gilani. My service has asked me to do a kind of 'fact-finding' mission, and you're one of several cabinet-level officials on our list."

"Yes, I suppose this sort of thing is necessary, although I'm not in favor of it. What sort of questions do you have in mind?"

"To be perfectly honest, I know very little about agriculture in Iran. But I've done some research, and I believe you'll be able to help us."

"Are you looking for evidence of corruption? Why else would our intelligence service ask you to come here?"

"That is one dimension. There are others."

"Okay, go ahead. I'm listening."

"First off, it's generally known that wheat, rice, and barley are our principal crops. I've eaten in many restaurants, and our basmati rice, in my opinion, must be the world's best."

"Yes, I would agree with that."

"But my research tells me that our government provides our famers with subsidies. With that money they're expected to buy special fertilizers and pesticides. And the government also guarantees they will receive a minimum price for their produce. To my service this sounds like socialism, and we know how that failed in the Soviet Union, not that many years ago."

"You may call it what you wish, but those decisions are not made in my ministry. They come from the ayatollah's cabinet.

And if you're looking for corruption, that would be a good place to begin looking."

"How is that?"

"It's simple. There are two cabinet ministers who follow agricultural production. They ensure that a farmer gets his guaranteed price, but at the same time, they charge our treasury an extra 15 percent, and that money goes right into their pockets. It's disgusting, but I'm powerless to intervene. And if you find that hard to believe, I suggest you drive by the homes that these men live in, every one a mansion, while one block away the residents live in two-bedroom flats."

"Could you name names, threaten to sue?"

"Not if I want to keep my job."

"Let's shift gears for a moment. Everybody knows that the finest carpets in the world are made here, in Iran. And, my research tells me, that is because we raise the best wool-producing sheep anywhere, with the possible exception of New Zealand."

"You're right about that. New Zealand's principal breed is the Merino. But not too long after our 1979 revolution we imported a number of Merino sheep from New Zealand, and now they're doing quite well, but only along the Caspian littoral where the climate is similar to New Zealand's. But our best producer is the so-called Asian Karakul, also known as the Persian lamb. This wool works best in caps and shawls. The Merino wool is used almost entirely in our carpet industry."

"Back to the corruption issue. Do you see that in the wool industry?"

"Unfortunately, we do. About 60 percent of all wool in Iran is sold at auction. In theory this is done with government supervision, but in practice it all too often doesn't work that way."

"Can you explain that?"

"Yes, easily. Let's say you're the auctioneer. Your bidders agree on the highest price, and you agree to that. But in order to get that highest price, their broker takes 10, maybe 15 percent for doing nothing but showing up at the auction. And the broker then shares maybe 5 percent with the government guy who is supposed to be making sure everything is legal. These people have been scamming the system for at least twenty years, and there's nothing my ministry can do about it."

"Hmm. I almost sympathize with you, sir. But I'm doing my job and you're doing yours. What you've told me is enough to satisfy my supervisor. And I thank you for your time."

* * *

This time Abdullah Safavi gave himself an A-minus. He now knew more about sheep and wool than he ever wanted to know. Still, it was solid evidence of more corruption, and his friends in Langley would want to know. As before, he went to his keyboard and made two copies of his report: one for his office and one for his iPhone. Washington would have his report in less than five minutes.

* * *

"Hey, Sam. Take a look at this. Another report from our man at VAJA."

"Just saw it. He's firing on all eight cylinders. But this report is long enough that I'm going to do a summary and send it off to Roya and Mustafa. She needs as much evidence as we can provide."

Nineteen

0830 hours, Monday, April 9, 2018, NSA Headquarters, room 4035.

"Hey, Jesse, you'd better come over here and have a listen."

"Sure, Huey, what's up?"

"Listen to this intercept. It's been unscrambled and translated from Farsi to English so we can understand it."

"So?"

"You'll remember that we got a request from the CIA about two months ago. They sent us a tape with two voices. We plugged that into our voice recognition software, and now this thing is a perfect match. It's a man and a woman; they're talking to each other on their cell phones."

"So why is this important?"

"The intercepting earth satellite records the exact location of the source. This is in Tehran, latitude 35.7622268 north, 51.418590 east. And I just checked that location with Google Earth, and guess what?"

"What?"

"It's a nightclub on Nelson Mandela Boulevard known as Jordan's Place."

"Hey, yeah, I *do* remember. We're supposed to log any conversations that come from that place."

"Okay, I'll switch on our speaker and we can listen in."

* * *

"Hussein? This is Fatima. I finally found your number and wanted to know how you're doing."

"Yeah, it's a tough grind, this rehab business. But I promised my dad I'd do it. He reminded me that people were beginning to gossip about my visits to Jordan's Place, so I decided to quit the joint and try to get straight."

"I'm proud of you for doing this, Hussein. I know our relationship has had its ups and downs, but if you stick with it, we should be fine."

"The worst part is these withdrawal pains. The clinic nurses give me some stuff, and that helps. They claim that within two more months I should be free to leave this place and go home."

"*I know it's a touchy subject, but how are things with your sister Roya?*"

"*Yeah, believe it or not, she came to visit me the other day. Before she left, we were both crying and hugging each other. I apologized for being so mean to her for so many years. She said she forgives me and not to worry about it. Then just as she was leaving, she said something I still don't understand.*"

"*What was that?*"

"*She said that within another month or so she expects 'big changes'— her words, 'big changes.' I'm not sure what she had in mind, but I suppose we'll find out.*"

"*Would it be okay if I come to see you, say tomorrow morning?*"

"Absolutely. I'd like that very much."

* * *

"That's it, Jesse, end of conversation. But I'm going to pipe this over to our friends in Langley. They'll know how to make sense of it."

Twenty

One more to go, then he'd be finished and his boss should be satisfied. This would be more difficult than the first two because his subject was one of the most influential men in the country. He decided he'd try to get an appointment with the country's Minister of Education, Armin Javadi. Same routine as before, ask his secretary to phone, tell the receptionist that a VAJA officer wants to interview the man, then wait for an answer.

* * *

"Yes, the minister can see Mr. Safavi at nine o'clock tomorrow morning. He'll be in his office, Tehran University, building six, first floor, room 1003."

* * *

"Thanks for agreeing to see me, Mr. Javadi. I know you're a busy man, and I promise this won't take long."

"Well, I should hope so. Why would VAJA want to talk to me? I've done nothing wrong, and the ayatollah knows that. I saw him just last week, and—"

"No, no, it's not *you* we're concerned about. It's the people who work for you. Look, my service is exploring the issue of corruption. It's a huge problem, and it's no longer a secret. Matter of fact, I was told the other day that an American newspaper, the *Wall Street Journal*, ran an article about corruption in Iran. The writer claimed that corruption is the main reason for our currency's collapse. The international banking community no longer trusts us to meet our obligations."

"Ah, yes. I'm afraid that's pretty close to the truth. Tell me, Mr. Safavi, what will VAJA *do* with whatever I tell you?"

"Our director will use it as part of a nationwide survey. When the survey is finished, he'll give it to the ayatollah's council of ministers, and they'll decide what to do. You're a member, so you'll be one of the first to know."

"Will you be using names, identifying the culprits?"

"Not necessarily, but that will be up to you and your colleagues on the council."

"Okay. That seems fair enough. First question?"

"Good. Everybody in the country knows that a good education—especially here, at Tehran University—is a surefire ticket to success. But we're not persuaded that the admissions process is fair. Say some high school guy from Khorasan Province applies for admission. His certified grade sheet shows a 3.7 GPA, and he wants to study international trade. Nobody ever heard of this kid, of course, and his application is denied.

"Then your admissions office receives an application from, say, a high school grad from Tehran's Imam Jaffar high school. His GPA is 3.3, and he gets in. But along with the application is a check, written by his father, for 100,000 rials. That money goes directly into the pocket of your chief admissions officer, and nobody knows about it."

"Is that hypothetical, or do you have evidence?"

"It's not hypothetical. VAJA has received written complaints about this, and the aggrieved parties are willing to testify.

"And I'll give you another example. Since the revolution we're supposed to be an equal opportunity country. In other words, women have the same rights as men have. But it doesn't work that way. A few months ago we received an email from a young woman, here in Tehran. Her name is Fatima Sheybani. She wants to study to become an actress and has already auditioned for several small theater groups. They like her work but have told her she needs a graduate-level degree to get a license. She applied to Tehran's Fine Arts/Theater academy and was turned down. She tried again, a month later, and included in the application a check, written by her brother, for 90,000 rials. Now she has her admissions certificate. Who has the 90,000? We don't know but whoever has it, if he or she is discovered, there will be big trouble, possibly an arrest."

"Yes, I see what you're driving at. Of course I know nothing about these matters because the perpetrators *don't want* me to know."

"That may be true, sir, but these crimes are being committed on your watch, and as the man in charge, you should be doing something to stop it.

"One last example, and then I'll leave you in peace."

"Yes, please do!"

"We both know there's a new construction contract out there. Your university wants to expand its campus to accommodate more students. The price of success, you might say. After the normal bidding process, that contract was given to the Ferdowsi Building Trust, the largest firm of its kind in Iran. It so happens that we have an informant on that company's payroll, and here's what he told us.

"He was in on the initial planning, and the company concluded that the contract was worth something like *fifty billion rials* over a five-year period. So how to secure the contract? Simple. There are three men on *your* board of directors, each one of them a good friend of Ferdowsi Building's CEO. The CEO calculated that getting the contract was worth at least one half of one percent of the contract value. So each of your three guys received something like 17 *million* rials in exchange for the contract. Now I'm not going to name names; that's up to you. But if word of this gets out, you, sir, might be looking for another job.

"Like I said, that's all. I'll file my report with my superiors and we'll see what happens."

* * *

Very good work, Abdullah! he told himself. As before, one copy to his supervisor and one copy into his iPhone. He tapped the send icon. In moments someone in Langley, Virginia, was about to be quite surprised.

Twenty-One

It had been a grueling week for Roya and Mustafa. So many calls from friends, from all over the country, but especially in Tehran and Mashhad. She was convinced she had their support, and Mustafa had taken an informal poll in the Grand Bazaar. Ninety percent of the merchants he had spoken to were in favor of their plan. And the encoded messages from Washington had convinced her it was time to act.

Now it was up to her to seek an appointment with her grandfather. It would be the most difficult thing she had ever done, but she knew there was no longer any room for doubt.

She left a message for the ayatollah's appointments secretary and asked him to return her call as soon as it was convenient.

* * *

"Ten o'clock tomorrow morning? Thank you. Please tell my grandfather I'm looking forward to seeing him again.

"Mustafa. Do you want to come with me or wait here?"

"Better I wait here, sweetheart. Many of those people who work at the palace don't approve of my being a Lebanese citizen. There's no point in reminding them that you married one."

* * *

At ten o'clock Roya was escorted into the ayatollah's library. He was the first to speak.

"It's good to see you again, my dear. It's been too long."

"Yes, it has. But I know how busy you are, and I wouldn't be here now, except that I have something important to discuss with you."

"Yes, I assumed so. Please, tell me."

"Grandfather, you have no reason to know this, but for the past year or so I've been talking to all kinds of people, all over the city. I've organized discussion groups, led by men and women who share my concerns. And there are people like me in Mashhad, Isfahan, Tabriz, Kerman, and even as far south as Bandar Abbas, who feel the same way."

"And how is that?"

"It's mostly about corruption, but there are other things, too. Rigged elections, dishonest members of the majlis, unfair dealings in the Grand Bazaar, investigations by VAJA that needlessly frighten people. I know for certain, for example, that three of your ministries—Finance and Banking, Agriculture, and Education—are taking bribes from the very organizations they're entrusted to supervise.

"In Khorasan Province, at least six cities are being led by dishonest politicians. We have the evidence to prove it.

"Even our Red Crescent volunteers are hearing complaints from their patients."

"Ah, yes. What you're telling me isn't surprising. My associates have said the same thing. You know, Roya, I'm approaching my eightieth birthday, and I feel my age. My predecessor warned me that the responsibilities of this office can be overwhelming, and he was right. But you didn't come here to tell me what I already know, or suspect. There must be something else."

"Yes, Grandfather, there is. I've spoken with my father—your son—about this, and he agrees with what I'm about to suggest."

"Go on."

"You know as well as anyone how much unrest and dissatisfaction there is out there among our citizens. In some places, I'm told, people are about to begin marching in the streets, demanding that our government do something. Probably the biggest concern is the value of our money; in the exchanges it's virtually worthless."

"Of course, I'm aware. But if you have a solution to offer, it had better be convincing."

"Yes, I—we—do. If you were to announce that you're turning over your office to your son, people would understand. They know that at your age such a decision makes sense."

"Yes, I would have to agree with that. And Habib has had enough experience to replace me. He's not well known, but he has never had to endure scandal of any kind, and his family is well liked. Your brother is an exception, of course, but he won't matter."

"No, Grandfather. Hussein and I have made up. He's in rehab right now and should be back on his feet very soon."

"Well, that *is* good news. I've been worried about your relationship with your brother for a very long time. But I'm sure you have some other ideas, as well."

"We do. This may sound radical, but we believe it's time to change the name of our country."

"Really? Well, now I *am* skeptical. You'll have to convince me."

"I believe I can do that. As you know, there are thirty provinces in Iran. Each one of them sends delegates to the majlis every four years. In other countries this is sometimes known as a *federation*. We believe we should rename our country the Islamic Federation of Iran. That name will satisfy the mullahs and other clergy and at the same time tell the world that Iran wishes to become more like other nations.

"And there's more. If you agree, Habib will announce some major policy changes. These are intended to help Iran rid itself of its terrible reputation as a sponsor of international terrorism. Here's the list we've agreed to:

"One. We'll publicly announce our intention to abandon our nuclear and guided missile programs and invite the international inspection teams to come here every six months.

"Two. Our nuclear program will be limited to the production of electric energy, first for Tehran and later for other major cities.

"Three. We will renounce our anti-Israel position and invite the Israelis to open an embassy in Tehran; and if the Americans wish, we'll send an ambassador to Washington.

"Four. We'll tell the Russians that we no longer will support their presence in Syria and that the al-Assad regime in Damascus will no longer receive help from us. Likewise, in Lebanon we'll withdraw our support of Hezbollah.

"Five. Our diplomatic service will focus on negotiating treaties with the European Union and the United States and Canada. These treaties will facilitate fair trade practices to encourage the free flow of goods and services."

"You know, Roya, I'm a tired old man. I've done my best which, obviously, hasn't been good enough. So, yes, I endorse your program, and you have my permission to tell Habib I said so."

Later that same day Mustafa phoned his wife's story to CIA headquarters.

Epilogue

Two months later, in the Oval Office. President Oglethorpe is speaking to CIA director David Franklin.

"Well, David, it seems your people pulled it off. Less than a year ago I asked you to arrange for—what was it?—*regime change*, that's what it was. And last week the whole world learned that Iran has a new government and a new name. They even want to open an embassy here in Washington. And I'm inclined to tell them they're more than welcome."

"Thank you, Mr. President. It took some time and the cooperation of a number of very smart and dedicated people.

For me, the most significant news is that their new president—
Habib Khamenei—has renounced the country's support of
international terrorism. They've promised to give up their
nuclear program, and they intend to restore relations with Israel.

"The Russians won't like it, but it looks as though they're out
of the game. That al-Assad butcher is on his own now. And
Hezbollah will soon run out of money."

"Yes, and I heard from our ambassador at the United Nations
that Habib Khamenei has asked that the sanctions be lifted
temporarily. They've also talked to the European Union, and
the EU has agreed to a temporary halt. We'll wait six months,
and if the Iranians do what they're promising to do, then we
can remove the sanctions permanently."

"And we're seeing that foreign investors are rushing in, seeking
new opportunities. Everything from beluga caviar, to pistachio
nuts, basmati rice, and Persian carpets. And oil, especially oil.
Already British Petroleum and Shell Oil are negotiating new

contracts. That, in turn, has restored the market's confidence in the rial, already up 900 percent from one week ago."

"David, there's another element to this story that intrigues me. This young woman, Roya. She's Habib's daughter, and she's been put in charge of a new social welfare program. They want to identify and provide government assistance to all the country's homeless, men *and* women. And it's to be financed from Iran's oil production revenues. That seems like a lot of responsibility for one so young. What do your people know about her?"

(At this point, director Franklin, recalling that his agency's most sacred duty is to protect its sources and methods, lied to the president.)

"Yes, Mr. President. We know that she's not yet thirty but other than that, not much. Although she does seem to be a very determined woman."

About the Author

©Yuen Lui Studio, 2003

John Sager is a retired United States intelligence officer whose services for the CIA, in various capacities, spanned more than half a century. A widower, he makes his home in the Covenant Shores retirement community on Mercer Island, Washington.

Printed in the United States
By Bookmasters